E.K. LARSON-BURNETT

the BEAR & the Rose

Springtide's reign:
death's domain.

The Bear & the Rose

Copyright ©2023 by E.K. Larson-Burnett

Cover illustration ©2022 by Nox Benedicta

Cover design ©2022 by E.K. Larson-Burnett

Edited by Brittany Corley

For Andrew, my soothing thing,

and for Cole, my brightness.

To the anxious pickers,

those with restless fingers.

You're warriors, all.

PRONUNCIATION GUIDE
in order of mention

Hazelfeur	*hay-zel-fear*
Artio	*are-tee-oh*
Rhoswen	*rose-when*
Púca	*poo-kuh*
Onora	*oh-nor-uh*
Nathaire	*nuh-tire*
Èilde Saibh	*ail-deh sigh-vuh*
Èilde Malvynn	*ail-deh mal-vin*
Èilde Diarmuid	*ail-deh deer-mid*
Dagda	*dahg-duh*
Danu	*dah-noo*
Bairnhart	*behrn-hart*
Maira	*may-ruh*
Dìomath	*dee-oh-mah*
Aengus	*ayn-gus*
Áine	*on-yeh*
Katelia	*kuh-tell-ya*
Teniélín	*ten-yell-een*
Morrigan	*mor-ee-gun*
Ràithne	*rah-nyeh*
Asrai	*ash-ray*
Éamon	*ay-mon*

Gobby	*guh-bee*
Lugh	*loo*
Finín	*fin-een*
Cernunnos	*kerr-noon-os*
Naoise	*nee-sheh*
Caoimhe	*quee-vah*
Anwena	*an-when-uh*
Mathúin	*ma-hoo-in*

Bear's
BANE

They once called me the Bear-Killing Maiden of Hazelfeur—a mouthful of a title, begot by little more than a penchant for stumbling upon the spawn of Artio at springtide.

In truth, I prefer Bearslayer.

I wear my accolade proudly, my neck graced with a mantle of oiled pelts and my hair knotted with dusky wraith bones, though it was by the crows' whimsy that I fell into the She-Bear's lair ten equinoxes ago. I was bare-shouldered then, and looked a maiden, even as I returned to Hazelfeur dripping ebon blood like tree sap, my imbrued scythe dangling from a frayed rope clenched so tightly in my moon-white fist that they couldn't prise it away from me, not even after I found sleep.

Now? Now I am no maiden.

I am Rhoswen, Thornfury's mistress, slayer of bears living and dead.

*T*he púca have always made my skin crawl. They occupy a far corner of the village at its highest point and in its biggest structure, a horned stone temple encircled by flowering hazel trees and traces of the sacrifices left to invoke the sprites' benevolence—broken stalks of grain, nutshells, wraithblood stains, tufts of fur.

I drop an ichor-slick antler at the foot of the temple. It rolls to a stop in the patch of sunlight between the shadows of the horns' prongs, and, preceded by a mere tremble of wind, it is snatched up by a cloven hoof.

"Bearslayer," says the púca, its voice a rattle of gravel upon my eardrums. It towers against the woven tapestry strung from the spires of the temple, a grisly goatish beast with a greasy beard and beaded eyes of molten gold, lip curled in a greedy sneer. It turns the antler between its hooves. "An untimely share."

"The sun hasn't yet slept," I counter, grinding a nutshell beneath my heel.

The púca eyes the sky, then licks the antler's length with a warted tongue and considers briefly. "A dawn's harvest."

I don't deign to give a reply.

"Springtide draws near. You must be busy preparing, little warrior rose." Its tongue draws the antler into its mouth, down its throat. "Gratitudes."

I offer a tight-lipped smile, resisting the urge to swallow. "Thornfury's pleasure. Until next hunting."

As I sketch a bow and turn away, the púca lets out a scraping laugh, but unwilling to be goaded or warned of Artio's spite, I march back to the village, brushing braided sprigs of bearsbane from my face. It's near sunsleep, and villagers are drawing instruments from their homes for the evening's festivities—the welcoming of spring.

I feel an unusual pulse of anxiety for the equinox, one I've not felt since before my legendary return from Artio's lair. Tonight my unease will beat in tune with the drums, and I resolve to stamp out its flame as we stamp our feet to prepare the ground for the coming season's bounty. I cannot allow it to fester, nor dwell on its meaning.

"Rhoswen!"

The call stops me before I can duck into my dwelling. The village healer—a snake-hipped woman named Onora— hurries my way, the painted glass in her hair clacking as she stops in front of me. She purses her lips as she studies my face. "Where is your brightness?" she demands, thumbing my cheek. The pad of her finger comes away smudged with deer blood and charcoal, and she holds it up for me to see.

"Up my arse," I say, shoving her hand away with a grin.

She sniffs; the wrinkling of her nose creases the swirls

of saffron smeared on its gently sloped bridge. "Come. You smell."

I let her powder-soft hand take my grimy, calloused one, and she leads me to her hut, where she wrestles Thornfury from my grip.

"He's family," I protest, grabbing for the worn leather strap as she winds it around the curved blade.

"Not my family. You know he int suitable for children, Rhoswen," she rebukes me, tucking Thornfury safely inside a basket at the roundhouse's opening.

Reluctantly I leave my weapon, the weightlessness at my hip unfamiliar, and follow Onora inside, where her fair-haired children shuck dead leaves from twigs and weave them into crowns. They giggle as I enter, tiny and impish hands darting out to touch the bearskins hanging from my shoulders before Onora shoos them away.

"Sit," she commands, ignoring my quirked brow to busy herself with bowls of powder and paint. The oldest of her children—a girl, freckled and pink—joins her, grinding dried petals to dust with nervous fervor. Another of the girls, at her mother's behest, takes up a bristled rind, dips it in oil from the crushed seeds of tulsi berries, and attacks my skin with it.

"Aye!" I exclaim, surprised at her force, and she gives me an apologetic look but scrubs all the more furiously, stripping grime and blood and impurity from every pore and hair she can reach.

"D'you ever bathe, Rhoswen?" Onora asks, taking up a

brush herself and coating my legs with the thick, sickly-sweet oil.

"Haven't the time, you ungrateful tuber. Too busy keeping your wee spuds uneaten." I snap my teeth at the wispy child, and she startles several steps backwards. "That's enough of that rancid stuff."

With the scrubbing settled, Onora takes up a bowl of paint, dips her fingers into it, and daubs it onto my forehead as Katelia, the older girl, watches. She murmurs softly as her fingertip swirls across my brow, perhaps praying, perhaps teaching. I don't pay her words much mind.

My thoughts drift to the coming days. Springtide ushers in a season of bloom and fertility, but it also heralds the season of the bear—Artio's season, one which she rules over with relentless vengeance. I've heard old tales of the goddess, tales from when she was green to motherhood, young and tender and forgiving, but it is hard to imagine such a thing when my knowledge of her is shrouded in red. She wishes to make the people of Hazelfeur suffer, and her army of bears, material and spectral, make ever-nearer attacks on our village.

This coming spring, I fear death.

I leave when every inch of my skin is gilded with Onora's "brightness"—my cheekbones dulled by labyrinthine whorls and the harsh ridge of my nose eased by mildly swirling motifs, golden clay caked in my lashes and packed under my fingernails, my arms and legs made to look as if they were tangled in silky vines.

There's a beauty to it, but I don't think any pantheon of gods would be swayed to bring more rain or sun by pretty smears of paint.

With Thornfury returned to his proper place on my belt, I skirt the rising bustle of the village, slipping mostly unnoticed to the garden behind my hut, where bushes of bearsbane shiver in the cool breeze. I haul a heavy sack to the middle of the garden and squat to strip stalks of needles from the bushes, braiding them deftly into thick garlands, the sharp smell stinging my nostrils. I work quickly, tucking into the sack strings of varying lengths to pass out at the springtide revels—long ones to string around fences, small ones for our necks, clippings to scatter across the ground.

By the time the sun has retreated from the horizon, my

fingertips are raw and my eyes are glazed. My mind, for a while having been blessedly preoccupied, rumbles with bloated worries that reverberate in my chest and teeth.

Springtide draws near.

The thrum of the drums begins at moonswake, and the center of the village is alight with dancing fire and painted bodies. Women in want of children dance naked, and men in want of women drum faster. Children offer strands of their hair to the flames and whistle with blades of grass pressed to their lips, attempting to coax piskies from their burrows.

I am late to the festivities, having bequeathed a branch of bearsbane to the púca in grudging compliance with the Pact of Hazelfeur—petty offerings from every harvest, no matter how small, and in return, peace from the mischievously-inclined sprites. A crude deal on our harebrained ancestors' behalf, and one I curse every time I visit the horned temple.

In the spirit of springtide, I decided not to deposit the harvest of my bowels at the púca's feet when it emerged to collect the bearsbane.

Now I sit by a fire, waiting for Nathaire—my hunting partner and occasional bedwarmer—to emerge from the shadows. I sip mulled tulsi wine brought to me by young villagers in exchange for bearsbane necklaces, and the honey-sweet burn in my throat assuages the icy loneliness gnawing at my insides; the loneliness that comes with being Bearslayer. When it comes to my presence, men turn to disdain, their pride threatened by my strength, while girls I once hoped to trade secrets with regard me with muddled expressions of respect, fear, and disgust, for which I can hardly fault them.

They tend hearths and nurse babes; I kill bears and thread bones into my hair.

I spy the village elders, the three of them blasély reclined around a distant fire, drinks slopping over their knees as they laugh primly at the whooping children. All of them are creatures of *sameness*, their movements and expressions and appearances unchanged in all the years I've lived—Èilde Saibh with her sheet of hair brushing the ground, Èilde Malvynn with his simple sky-blue tunic, Èilde Diarmuid with their mouthful of rudiwhit root. As I watch them speak merrily of the weather's inclinations, I wonder if their thoughts are truly as simple and unworried as they appear.

One of Onora's daughters—the middle one, Teniélín, her circlet of twigs askew—bounces up to me, eyes bright, the flush of her round cheeks hidden under shimmering trinities of wheat-gold spirals. She extends a delicate hand, fingers still plump with youth.

"Come, dance for the Dagda!" she says, trying to pull me to my feet.

Surprised by the lack of hesitancy in her invitation and

limbs loosened by the wine, I oblige, letting her tug me into the clouds of dust and smoke and bodies undulating amid the bonfires. Laughter froths from my throat as I move freely, enjoying the recklessness of dancing, so unlike hunting, where each movement is calculated, careful.

Teniélín clasps my hands, then flings her arms sideways, impelling me to spin; my hair falls loose from its knot at the base of my skull and swirls around me, bone shards rattling.

And I suddenly feel like vomiting.

I twirl the girl with enough force that she's swallowed by the springtide fray, and I take the opportunity to slip away, backing into the shadows. Out of sight, I stagger, land on my knees, and choke on breaths that come too quick.

Almost instantly I feel a hand on my back, its feathery touch familiar. Nathaire has found me—to bear witness to my falling apart, as is his custom. He drags my heavy pelts away so the breeze can kiss the back of my neck.

He leans forward so I can see him, and his fingers, bright with bronze powder, flash a question.

"*Goldroot?*" he signs, and I nod jerkily. He wedges his hand in my armpit and steers me gently toward my hut.

"I—despise—springtide," I say between gasps, wildly scraping my hair from my sweat-sticky face as we hurry through the darkness. "Could the Dagda not abandon his harp for a single equinox? Could we not dance for him next moon—"

Nathaire stops, circles my wrists with his fingers, and draws my hands to his bare chest, where powder has clotted with sweat. He releases me, letting me scratch at the flaking bronze while he signs, *"Tell it to the bees, Roz."*

I stand still for a moment, attempting to ease the heaving of my chest, invoking the image of the winged insects carrying my worries up to the heavens. It does nothing to settle the mounting pressure. I stifle a scream and pinch my chalky fingertips, three hard squeezes each. Then I scowl and swat Nathaire away. "Bees, gods, you—no one listens."

"If I could stop the seasons from changing, I would." He turns, walking sideways so I can read his hands. *"The Dagda will play his harp this moon whether we ask it or not. It is his nature, as it is ours to dance, as it is the flowers' to bloom."*

"That's hardly a comfort."

"It wasn't meant to be."

We enter my hut and Nathaire rekindles the fire at its heart, setting over the gentle flames a pot of water for goldroot tea, the leaves for which he extracts from a pouch at his thigh.

I begin to pace, my feet treading the worn path of packed earth that curves around my hearth. "We've hardly been able to keep the wraithspawn at bay past springs," I say with a hiccup. My lungs seize and seize and seize. "When they and their living counterparts wake...Natty, Hazelfeur will be overrun. Our men are not warriors."

But Nathaire already knows this. He says nothing as he pinches silken goldroot strands into a bowl.

I collapse into the pile of furs and grouse-feather cushions against the wall where I sleep.

16

"I am so tired," I murmur, my voice rising as my stomach drops ever lower.

Nathaire pours heated water over the goldroot and twists the bowl carefully. The swirling water becomes amber, and steamy tendrils carry a pleasant aroma to my nostrils. He lifts the bowl to his lips, and his two malformed tongues—the source of his muteness—dart out to catch the sweet moisture.

He presses the bowl into my hands and signs, *"As am I."*

Then he settles beside me in the furs and begins coiling the long lengths of my hair into tight knots.

I nurse the goldroot tea down to its dredges.

While I was born to no family, Nathaire was born with two tongues.

He was not birthed in Hazelfeur, or so it is assumed, but was quickly abandoned to our village before he even had the chance to open his eyes. The healer that came before Onora—of whom I remember nothing but silvered ropes of hair and the smell of citrus—found him nestled under the púca's hazel trees, an infant with the stumpy, forked tongues of a demon.

Much of our village believes he is cursed, but the luckier women of Hazelfeur find his deformity quite a blessing.

I, too, have occasionally been a lucky recipient of Nathaire's curse.

We share love, though not the sort that bears children; only tender friendship and raw, visceral lust. He provides other women children, but I neither envy nor desire such things.

I don't believe Danu would grant me children even if I asked, for how can a motherless girl become a mother?

N athaire finishes pinning my hair with tiny spears of bone, and his fingers work their way from my scalp to my neck, his whisper touch sending thrills sparking behind my ears. I cast aside my bowl and lean into him, allowing him to take from me the weight of my body while the goldroot takes the oiliness from my core—my soothing things, this boy and his tea.

I will not celebrate springtide, but I will be distracted from it.

Nathaire's callouses scrape against the bony knob at my nape, his stubbled chin grazes my shoulder, and I sigh, expelling with my breath the lingering thoughts of horned wraithbears. As his hands travel down my arms and his lips find my jaw, my rigid muscles become liquid and I forget of the drums that beat and beg for the end of winter.

No, I realize, I did not forget the drums—their sound has ceased, and in their place, my people scream.

The bears have already awoken.

I spring to my feet, Thornfury in my fist, and Nathaire is at my heels with his bow and quiver as I sprint back into the night.

Villagers flee into their roundhouses, children dragged by their limbs, their clothes, their hair. Women frantically toss bearsbane garlands across thresholds and men wield unsharpened sticks with wild eyes.

"Inside," I tell them, and they obey without ever having intended otherwise.

Nathaire and I follow the screams, running toward the eastern edge of the village, nearest Bairnhart Forest, where daub and splinters of wood spray into the air. As we near, a girl slams into me and collapses, naked, bloody, and sobbing. With little tenderness, I haul her up by the arm and shove her in the direction of Onora's home. Nathaire looses a sliver-thin arrow; it whizzes past a half-crushed hut and buries into the matted brown breast of the season's first fleshbear.

Though fleshbears are easier to kill, they are bigger than the wraithbears, have not yet experienced death, and possess the maternal protectiveness that urges them to attack all the more furiously.

I despise the beasts.

The lone fleshbear roars, swipes at the arrow shaft protruding from its fur, and lumbers toward us, on its way completing the decimation of the hut from which the bloodied girl fled.

Nathaire takes aim and I dart sideways, sweeping my leg through the dirt in an arc as I swing my arm wide, flicking Thornfury's chain, letting the scythe slice through the meat of the bear's flank.

The momentum jerks the handle nearly free from my fingers, which are slick with oil and paint. "Danu's *tits*, Onora!" I growl, just catching the leather before it's out of my grip.

The bear, its teeth-rattling roar unrelenting, veers to face me head-on. The green feathers of Nathaire's second arrow bloom grotesquely from its eye socket, and I quickly slip into the new blind spot. With a flick of my wrist, Thornfury flashes through the air and the blade cuts through the soft flesh of the bear's belly, and with another flick catches a glance of moonlight and falls silently upon the back of her neck. I snap the chain and catch Thornfury as the beast's severed head drops into the dirt.

"*Glorygoat*," Nathaire signs, but I have no time to explain that Thornfury is due for sharpening—a warbled wail rises from the rubble the bear left in her wake.

I scramble to the wreckage and sift through the mess of crumbled straw and dried mud until I uncover a leg, blessedly attached to the unclothed body of a young man on the cusp of unconsciousness.

His torso is gouged from collarbone to groin, none of his innards where they belong and some missing entirely, but his glassy eyes find me. "Maira..."

"Alive," I say.

He says no more but lowers his chin a fraction, and I plunge Thornfury into his throat.

Moonsleep passes without mercy and Maira's cries for her beloved carry through sunswake. She stands alone in the field, hunched like a wilted flower, weeping. Occasionally she lifts her gaze to the towering Sun Stone where the corpse rests. Trembling fiercely, she watches the crows strip his bones clean.

As I watch the grief consume her with a hollow ache in my throat, my fingers work on their own, twisting and braiding. Coarse hair from the boy, a claw from the bear. I string them both around my neck.

He was the first—gone before the first day of spring had even fully dawned.

athaire and I leave the village to hold cautious vigil closer to the forest, a springtide ritual we've made grim habit of and in which we take no joy. We trample a solemn path in the long grass at Bairnhart's treeline, silent but for the dull chime of Thornfury's chain and the hollow clatter of Nathaire's arrows in their quiver.

After hours of anxious pacing and no movement from within the rousing forest, I grow sick of idling.

"The elders must be persuaded to take action," I say, as I've said every equinox. The elders have always refused to abandon Hazelfeur, even in more recent years as the bears grew bolder and began breaching the village. Even now that a boy has died. They put too much value on their bargain with the púca; they insist that the sprites' goodwill may not extend beyond the borders of the scrublands.

Nathaire scratches his head at length, aware as I am that the elders are deaf when it comes to notions of change. "*Perhaps your insufferable insistence is key,*" he signs, and we return to the village with weapons unbloodied.

I find Èilde Saibh sitting under the yet-unbloomed

branches of the hawthorn tree, its deadened limbs casting shadows across her face. She smiles as I approach as if I am a warm breeze after a storm. Her insouciance infuriates me.

"You are aware that our village is plagued by Artio's bearspawn?" I ask of her, plucking viciously at the wiry hairs of my eyebrow to keep the anger occupied.

She only blinks, unruffled.

"The beasts pose infinitely more threat than the púca and their gut-brained Pact." I feel a childish scorch of shame at my language in front of the elder, and pluck my brow all the more fiercely. "What use is their amity if we're all dead?"

Èilde Saibh shakes her head. Hammered coins jingle too merrily in her hair. "There are intricacies to the Pact we cannot understand, Bearslayer," she says. "Our púca weave meaning into their words that we cannot hope to make sense of. Leaving Hazelfeur could also mean death."

"Can we not renegotiate the terms?" I finger the gnarled claw beneath my tunic and feel a similar hardness form in my gut. "A boy died, Saibh. Something must be done."

"We are bound by our ancestors' word." She says it dismissively, then casts her milky gaze skyward. "She will find solace here, our Maira, under the tender-hearts' tree."

"As will your husband, when more of Artio's children wake," I snap—a warning? a promise?—and turn away, leaving the elder to her tree-pondering.

I fret about the village restlessly, stringing bearsbane, honing Thornfury's blade, helping clear the debris where Maira's beloved breathed his last, until finally I stomp to the hazel tree grove and stand before the darkness at its center.

I bite my tongue, spit blood at the temple's shadow.

The púca is there in a breath, this time a dark-furred creature with peaked ears and banded aureate eyes—whether it's the same sprite that wore a goat's head before, I cannot know; the púca shapeshift, and I have never seen them take the same form twice.

"Bearslayer blood," the leporine púca drawls, toeing the glob of saliva. "We are not demons to be summoned, warrior rose."

Heedless, I spit again. "If you wish to continue receiving Hazelfeur's harvests, you will divulge the terms of the Pact. If we were to leave, would we be hunted by your kind?"

The púca cocks its head. "Were you to leave. Suddenly fearful of the bearfolk, are you?"

"I am but one Bearslayer."

"And did you not vow to be Hazelfeur's sole protector?"

I hesitate, thinking of that night I ceased to be just a girl with no father or mother—*I shall be Artio's bane,* I had sworn to the elders, *and Hazelfeur's living protection.* Bold words meant only to ensure my place in the village, vowed before I realized the gravity of what protecting a home entailed—blood, uncertainty, estrangement. In hoping to obtain a family, by proving my worth I lost any chance of one.

"Bear-killing is not the only way I can protect them," I say finally, losing some of my daring.

"Mmm," replies the púca. Its liquid eyes simmer, betraying no emotion. "We do not hunt on whim alone."

"Speak plainly."

Its lip curls. "To do so is not our whim, either."

I fist my hands at my sides, my throat constricting with warring waves of frustration and desperation, wondering momentarily what villagers boast relation to the elders who made the Pact and imagining my foot so far up their arse that their ancestors can feel it.

"I look forward to your next offering, Bearslayer," the púca says with a lazy flick of its paw, and it leaves me and my sacrifices of spit.

When I turn, I find Nathaire watching from beyond the tight-budded hazel trees. He's wiped clean of the smeared springtide paint I last saw him in, his expression unreadable as his fingers idly knead his scalp.

"Those spudheaded *púca,*" I snarl without greeting. "You're lucky the healer found you before *they* did."

He huffs a laugh. "*I am not entirely certain they did not,*" he signs, afterward gesturing to his mouth.

I blink, startled despite his bemused expression. The thought that the púca gave him his two tongues had never crossed my mind, though asking them would do nothing for the uncertainty.

"*I do not need to know,*" he signs, reading my face. Then, "*You haven't slept.*"

"The village needs better defenses. But to need wood for fencing means to need men in the forest. And these men..."

I trail off as one of the men we speak of comes from the village with a bushy handful of unwashed fulcress bulbs. He acknowledges me with a jerky nod, then continues up the rise to lay the bulbs in front of the temple. A púca with a crested mane of strange barbs appears to collect the offering, but the man doesn't linger to engage and hurries down the path, back into the village.

"*These men are farmers, Roz. Fearful ones.*" Nathaire shakes his head, copper glinting in the dark coils that slip from behind his ears. "*They would not fight a cock if it crowed in their face.*"

"They need to be taught," I admit, "but there's no time. Spring hardly waited, and there will be no reprieve until next equinox."

"*We could petition the elders to enforce a patrol just outside the village. We could be better prepared.*"

"We could," I agree, but we both know the elders aren't likely to entertain any idea involving the removal of their wrinkled arses from their seats.

But I am not a woman of inaction, with an itch in my blood which I fancy I inherited from a wild-hearted mother—perhaps a dancer, or a traveler—and in my head crystallizes a conviction that I have dismissed many times, an inevitability that has beckoned me—*taunted* me—since I emerged from Bairnhart Forest as the Bear-Killing Maiden.

I must return to the belly of the beast that made me.

I must seek out the source of Hazelfeur's woes, the mother of all bears.

I must slay Artio.

The thawing forest imparts no intimation of the horrors that call it home. Light trickles between the trees, warming the fallen leaves and needles, illuminating languidly drifting motes that wink in and out of sight.

Though it seems peaceful, I know this place can shatter serenity in a heartbeat. Artio's wraithbears do not sleep, and her fleshbears are unpredictable. They could break through the shafts of brightness without warning, gory maws unhinged and bloodlust blazing in the voids of their eyes.

What inspires Artio to mother such vicious aberrations—so unlike the flighty beasts of hunt whose sole motive is self-preservation—remains an enigma. As Nathaire often reminds me, such is the way of the gods.

But I know there are other answers.

I move quietly, favoring the balls of my bare feet, though the wetness of the ground softens any noise I may make. Nathaire creeps stealthily through the foliage, undetectable even to me, a shadow in all but the blood that warms him. I didn't try to dissuade him from accompanying me. Had I the fight in me, he still would have come.

I lead us into the trees, deeper than we usually venture. We spend most of our days watching the treeline, accosting threats far from the village, or hunting in the sparser woods that feed into Bairnhart.

Artio's lair, though, lies at the heart of the forest.

I can hardly believe I'm returning, eleven equinoxes having passed in a blaze. I had been alone then, and it had been night, several hours past sunsleep. The moonlight hardly allowed for sight, but it didn't matter; I didn't know where I was going—I knew it only after what felt like hours, when I stumbled and fell. I remember little beyond that. I hit my head in the fall and broke several ribs, and the simple handheld scythe I had brought, tied to a length of rope, wrought a gash through my eyebrow. There was darkness and pain and a not-unpleasant smell that still haunts me.

And then the bears woke, mighty presences I could not see, only feel, and a voice soothed, *"It is not time yet, my rose."*

My memories after fade into inky crimson, leaving me doubtful it was truly Artio's lair I fell into—but what else could have transpired, if not my awakening as her bane? I bathed in her spawn's blood that night; I started a war against her that will end this day.

We stop to rest, Nathaire forcing a dried strip of meat into my mouth that I promptly vomit back up, my belly too upset by a serpentine writhing.

"You should have stayed in the village," I tell him, dragging the back of my hand across my lips. "They need protection, especially now. Retreat to the treeline. Make tea for my return."

His brows draw together, and his gaze meaningfully drops to where my fingers pluck the hair from my arms.

I press my anxious fingers to his chin. "Please, Nathaire."

He nods, reaches up to squeeze my wrist. *"Rain fury on her,"* he signs, a soft gravity in the movement of his hands. He disappears into the trees.

And then I am alone.

I resume my journey through the forest, and the sun resumes its course through the sky, its light glaring more harshly as if to urge me to turn back.

When I hear a flurry of footsteps, I strangle Thornfury's strap in the vise of my fist, knowing Nathaire would never be so reckless as to make such noise. I turn in a circle, the coiled muscles in my calves thrumming. The trees stand still and unruffled, but they are not the only things that live here, and I will not be fooled.

The patter of feet this time is accompanied by a flash of verdancy at the edge of my vision. I take pursuit, but find myself chasing air and stop abruptly, wondering if I'm being baited by a tricky piskie.

A laugh like bells floats from behind me, twinkling in my ears.

I whirl around just as a fleshbear explodes from the brush.

A claw swipes inches from my face, avoided only by my falling on my backside. Momentarily jarred by the beast's frosty green eyes, the following swipe snags the woolen cloth of my tunic where it billows at my hip. I roll away, scrambling to my feet, and snap Thornfury's chain—a desperate swing, one which falls pitifully short as I slip in the muck left by winter's end.

The bear surges forward and a razor-sharp claw clips my shoulder, again flattening me against the ground. With an unintelligible curse directed at a god I'm not sure exists, I swing my scythe wildly, hacking at nothing as the bear lurches a safe distance away. I find my footing, shift my grip from the scythe's handle to the chain, and, for a strange moment, lock gazes with the bright-eyed beast.

Neither of us move. Both our chests heave.

When I'm certain it has been far too long since my

heart's last beat, I crack Thornfury like a whip, aiming for the bear's heart, watching the crescent blade glide through the fur of its hind leg instead.

I didn't see it move, only noticed a nearly imperceptible shiver of light in the air around it before Thornfury struck far from his mark. Frowning, trying to comprehend some trick of the sun, I simply stand there as the bear turns and flees.

I shake my hesitation and dash after the bear, but it leaves no trace of its flight —not a drop of blood, not a single crushed leaf.

The She-Bear is baiting me. She knows I'm here, perhaps even what I'm here for, but rather than face me she forces her spawn to toy with me, tire me.

"You would send your children to fight for you?" I call into the trees, feeling suddenly exposed, suddenly angry. "You would send them to *die* for you?"

A response comes, but not one I expected—a girl's cry, a scream of fear morphing into a strangled bleat of pain. It sounds distant, but I am certain it comes from the direction that the bear fled, and I launch into movement.

There is someone out here with me and Artio's monsters. A tree-worshipper? A traveling faerie? No person from Hazelfeur lacks brains enough to venture into Bairnhart, and I refuse to wonder if I will lose another of my people. I cannot lose another.

I break into a clearing and nearly don't see her huddled at the base of an alder tree, skidding to a halt only when I hear her breathy whimper. I feel a stutter of relief when I don't recognize her, and then a gasp of it when the area proves clear of bears. I hook Thornfury to my belt and rush to the girl's side, realizing quickly she's more woman than girl—and more beautiful than I thought a woman could be.

Her eyes are pinched shut and her skin is pale as ash, but she seems to radiate warmth and softness, her features delicate but her posture strong, regal almost, even though she is clearly suffering. Entranced beyond my understanding, I have to force my eyes from her face to find the source of her pain. My fingers flutter to her thigh, where a scarlet patch blooms through her dress. I tug at the fabric—beneath it, her skin is softer than anything I've ever touched, and the liquid sensation steals a sigh from my lungs.

Startled at my touch, the girl opens her eyes, her irises spring's greenest hue, and instantly I find myself unsteadier than I can ever recall feeling, dizzied by the pools of fallen heavens shining from her face, and I don't think even Nathaire's goldroot tea could help me breathe now.

"You're hurt," I say dumbly.

"You're not a bear," she says in reply.

We both laugh stiffly.

I return my attention to her wound, the ugliness of it at odds with its bearer. Pressing my lips together to keep from grimacing, I swab away the oozing blood with the torn edge of my tunic—though her dress is already stained beyond saving, I can't bring myself to soil it any further. The gash is deep but not ragged as I expected it to be.

"A bear attacked you?" I ask, frowning.

For a moment her face is twisted by fury, her gaze on my mantle of pelts, but then she makes a tinny noise at the back of her throat and tears spring to her eyes. "It was—so fast—" She gasps, swallowing hard.

My stomach plummets at her distress, and my thumb brushes a crystal drop from her cheek before I can stop myself. I snatch my hand away at the widening of her eyes and croak an apology, again attempting to focus my attention on the still-bleeding gash. I press my palm against it, feeling the rapid *un un un* of her heartbeat in her leg, somehow slower than mine, which hammers relentlessly, *ununun*, flooding my face with heat.

I bow my head, fumbling with blood, fabric, and porcelain skin. "What are you doing out here? Where are you fr—"

I sense the wraithbear before the girl cries out; the whisper of brittle bones, the rush of icy air, the stinging miasma of rot.

Springing to my feet with Thornfury returned unbidden to my grip, I face the creature. It wavers before me, distorting the woods around it with an inky gloom, beaded tourmaline eyes suspended in gaping, sinewy sockets.

I lash out. The bearsbane tucked through the links of Thornfury's chain forces the wraith to the edge of the clearing but it advances again. Its cavernous maw gapes in a grisly scream as it rushes toward us, black ichor streaming down a bone-scabbed throat, scaled eyes bursting from below jagged horns, a recurring nightmare incarnate.

Again I lash out and the monstrous creature writhes clear of Thornfury's blade. Its screech reaches a pinnacle of noise that rattles my teeth, and it rushes me in a blur, but before I can plunge a fist of bearsbane into its yawning mouth, the girl seizes my arm and *pulls*, and I find myself falling in an all-too-familiar way.

"Danu's tits!" I shriek, slamming hard into packed earth. I stagger upright, bashing my head against a root-riddled ceiling, and drop to my knees instantly, disoriented by the sudden darkness.

The girl's cool hand presses against my lips, and from the oblivion her eyes gleam brightly, wide with terror, urging me to be quiet.

From above I hear the wraithbear's howl fade, the rasping of bones passing into the distance, and then silence.

"Apologies," the girl murmurs, drawing backwards so her head is haloed by a shaft of weak sunlight, a crown of gold rays woven into the silk brown of her hair. She peers through the hole we fell through, several yards above our heads.

I look around, unable to see much beyond walls of dirt and gnarled knuckles of roots punching through. Red fringes my vision, the blur of memory stealing into my head and reaching needle-sharp fingers into my lungs.

Artio's lair.

Wracked by panicked gasps, I begin clawing at the protrusions below the opening, trying to haul myself back to the surface, in my fear forgetting the reason I came to the forest.

"No, please!"

The girl's cry gives me pause. I turn, still hasting, and offer her my hand. "It isn't safe here," I say.

She takes my hand but tugs it, gently pulling me away from the light of safety. "I promise you it is. Please—I cannot leave."

I open my mouth to argue—*not safe, Artio's lair, I will protect you*—but the words are stolen away by the vision of her surrounded by a golden nimbus, the majesty of early sunsleep permeating her ashen skin with warmth, illuminating hidden constellations of freckles.

And I am unexplainably, irreversibly enchanted.

*T*he girl—my enchantress—promises she will explain why we're safe in what I am certain is the nest of Artio's children, but her leg still bleeds and I will not let her die first.

I wrap her thigh tightly with a strip torn from my tunic, but have nothing else to ease her discomfort or help the wound heal.

"I need to get you to my village," I tell her. "Our healer will help you."

She shakes her head, nut-brown ringlets trembling about her face. "I cannot leave. I tried, but I am bound here by my blood."

"Bound to the forest?" I ask. "I can protect you from the beasts."

"You can't," she insists. "Please..."

"Rhoswen," I supply, eager to hear it from her lips.

She smiles. "Rhoswen. Men have tried and failed to free me before. I don't wish their fate upon you."

"I am no man..." I wait for her name.

"Dìomath." The way she says it feels like a blessing.

"You're the woman Bearslayer. I've heard speak of you."

"Have you? I didn't know this forest had so many visitors."

Another lustrous shake of the head. She shifts her leg and whimpers. Sweat pearls on her brow.

I grind my teeth together. "I have to go to the village for supplies—but I will come back, Dìomath. I will come back for you."

She grasps for my hand as I stand, squeezes it, and smiles again.

It's all I need to run faster than I knew I could.

It is nearly moonswake by the time I reach Hazelfeur, and the village is still and quiet. Nathaire, who had awaited me at the treeline, tails me to Onora's hut wordlessly. I watched him scrutinize the blood on me as I emerged from the forest, and I know what he must think—that I succeeded in what I set out to do. I don't tell him otherwise, thankful he can't see the shameful flush under my skin; thankful he can't know I forgot my village's plight with just a glimpse of Dìomath's beauty.

Aengus's toenails, you weak thing, I scold myself.

I am still overcome by her beauty, the brightness of it imprinted on the backs of my eyelids. I have never wondered at my own appearance, never felt inspired by its effect on people, but Dìomath...she makes me want to be beautiful.

Impelled by haste to return to my forest-bound enchantress, I burst into Onora's hut, startling her children. Onora, braiding painstakingly painted beads into Teniélín's fair hair, abandons the intricate plait when she sees the blood on me.

"You're hurt," she says, but I shake my head.

"I need wrappings. And salve, healing salve, for a cut." I pause, my insides churning. "I may have to sew skin. How—what do I need for that?"

Nathaire touches my shoulder, furrowing his brows in question.

"A girl in the forest," I gasp. "She's wounded."

Onora does not ask any questions, only hurries to gather jars and pouches, passing them to the freckled older child, who settles them carefully into a basket. Then Onora takes up the basket and marches past me.

I frown, glancing to Nathaire before following her outside. I slip ahead of her and block her path. "Onora, I cannot allow you to accompany me. It isn't safe."

"You don't know how to sew skin, Bearslayer." She grabs my wrist and holds my hand up so it is illuminated by starlight. "For Áine's sake, woman, lookit your fingers."

Fingers crusted by dirt and blood, nails chewed to nubs. I feel my face redden. "I encountered two bears just today, *woman*. I can't allow you to come to the forest with me. I forbid it."

A fierceness I have only seen in mothers alights in her eyes, and she glares in a way that I fight to not wither beneath. Seconds pass before I fail and relent.

"Fine," I grunt, still reluctant. "Your children—can they be left alone?"

"They're children, not lambs."

"I don't know what that means...but we haven't the time

46

to discuss the strength of sheep. Come, the girl lost much blood."

She follows me out of the village, keeping pace all the way to Bairnhart's treeline. Hesitating briefly, she murmurs a prayer and touches a knotted length of thin rope at her throat, and then we plunge into the shadowed forest. Onora keeps her hand tucked in the crook of my elbow. She does not need to be told to stay quiet.

I lead as confidently as I can, though it is difficult to see the marks I hacked into the tree trunks in the darkness; I mistake the peeled crescents of bark for the sickeningly wet grins of nightmare beasts. Even more distracting are thoughts of Dìomath; her veiled green eyes, the bow above her lip, the supple curve of her cheek. She is a creature whose likeness I have never encountered before, not even in Onora—whose softness I have always envied—and not a trace of which could be found in the hard angles of Nathaire.

We break into the clearing where I found my enchantress earlier, our journey uninterrupted, and I softly call her name.

"I am here, Rhoswen," comes her answer. A voice like flowing water or honeyed bread—tempting, liquid warmth.

I help Onora into the hole in the ground, then pass her the basket and slip carefully into the hidden pocket, where this time the breath isn't knocked out of me by impact but by *her*.

Dìomath sits where I left her, hands still clasped tight

over her wound. Her unbound hair has been pushed back from her face with a crown of intertwined roots; it explodes behind her ears in a cascade of curls and puddles on the ground, the ends of it silvered by moonlight.

She looks past Onora, blinks at me, and I am swallowed whole.

Enchantress, I want to say, but I clear my throat and manage a croaky, "Alright?"

Dìomath nods. Her gaze flickers back to Onora, who has begun unloading her basket.

"Our village healer," I explain. "Her poultices smell like arse, but she's very good."

Onora snorts with disdain but I ignore it, entranced entirely by the giggle Dìomath tries to stifle. I would summon a wraithbear to my own roundhouse just to have such a laugh lull me to sleep.

Weak, selfish thing, I again think of myself.

"May I?" Onora kneels and gestures to the bloodsoaked fabric I cinched around the wound. Dìomath nods and Onora peels the bandage from her thigh. She glances at me, lips pursed, frowning. "This...this is hardly a cut, child. It needs no stitching."

Surprised, I peer over her shoulder at Dìomath's leg. The puckered wound is near impossible to discern in the dark, an inconsequential thing no longer than my smallest finger. I gape, certain it had been worse. "But—but the blood. There was so much, I thought—"

"For a Bearslayer, she's a squirmy one, int she?" Onora

huffs, no doubt regretting her stubbornness and mourning the moments lost with her little ones. "Lucky little maiden you are," she tells Dìomath, prodding the wound with gentle fingers. "I've seen the bears do much worse to Rhoswen."

"From what I've heard, she has delivered her revenge tenfold," Dìomath says. With her gaze averted, a tiny flutter of her eyelashes is all that betrays a glimpse of disarming vulnerability; of the tender heart hidden beneath her fragile bones.

Her quiet reaction stirs something in me, something at odds with the urge to defend my occupation—I do what I must to protect my people. It is all I know.

But perhaps there is more to know.

Perhaps it is this girl of the forest.

yearn to stay with Dìomath, but I know Onora cannot find her way back to Hazelfeur alone, and my enchantress assures me she will be safe in her hollow. As I bid her sweet rest, I see the promise in her eyes: should I come back, she will tell of her secrets.

Until then, I will dream of her.

We return to the village, again undisturbed by Artio's spawn, and I marvel at our good fortune. I wonder to whom Onora prays.

"Rhoswen." Onora squeezes my arm when we come to her hut. "That boy you hunt with...I saw him all about the village today. I don't notice him often. He's quiet as a shadow, int he?"

"Nathaire. I needed him here in my place. He's just as much a Bearslayer as I am."

"He brewed four pots of tea."

I laugh, but I am sobered by the thought of Nathaire keeping tea warmed all evening. "He cares for me, you nosy tuber. And I for him."

She scrutinizes my face, her eyes shadowed by an oily

smudge of umber across her brows and the luminescent designs adorning her eyelids.

"Not tonight, Onora," I sigh. "You know my heart and its lack of yearning for a husband. And Natty is too inclined toward wildness to dream of a wife."

"What of the girl?" she asks.

My mouth snaps open and shut, and I touch my cheeks to ensure they haven't taken fire. "The...girl?"

"Is she running from a man as well?"

"I don't know," I admit. I scratch my jaw and flakes of unwashed paint from springtide come away under my fingernails. "And I am *not* running from any man. For the most part, the men run from me. As they should."

Onora's gaze waxes heavenward and she shakes her head, but there's humor in the slant of her lips.

As she turns to part ways, I find my fingers tangled in the knots of my hair, blood-crusted bearsbane needles drifting to the ground. I know I must look a sight, and it's no wonder that, of the many emotions that alight in men's eyes when they see me, desire is not one of them. My throat tightens.

"Your daughters," I blurt after Onora. "Have they the stomach for a challenge?"

T he two older girls—Katelia and Teniélín—take bristles to my hair with determination and delight, bickering charmingly over which of them will remove the wraith bones from the tiny, scattered braids and which will hack away the parts clumped with unidentifiable substances, those matted beyond untangling.

Onora sits on the other side of the hearth, watching and guiding the girls while the youngest sleeps on her breast. She draws overlapping spirals onto her ankles and toes with a finger dipped in paint. Each stroke is practiced and smooth, and her movement does not disturb the sleeping child.

I sit as still as I can, but when the yanking on my scalp brings tears to my eyes, I yelp and pull away, warding the girls off as if they're armed. They might as well be with those brushes of theirs.

"Gently," Onora murmurs, and they heed her words, working more oil into the knots, unafraid of my scowl. I try to ignore the pity in her eyes as she watches chunks of fiery auburn clods fall.

I pluck one of the clumps from the ground and hold it up to the firelight with morbid fascination. "It hardly looks like hair. *Is it hair?* Gods. Goats have lovelier manes, aye?"

She winces. "You'd not be crying of the pain if you brushed your hair more often, heathen."

"My time is better spent sleeping than washing," I say—though I've never truly had much luck with either—and flick the mass of locks into the flames.

"Your hair smells worse than my salves."

"In that case, perhaps I should save the rest for the púca."

"Rhoswen, by the crows, you're not a child," Onora says, and though her tone is even, her voice quiet enough not to wake the child, I hear her exasperation. "Hazelfeur would look to you as a leader, but you've got *rot* on your head. Do you not care what we think of you?"

I pinch my fingertips—*onetwothree, onetwothree*—and focus on the twinge of pain at my scalp. Gritting my teeth and wishing my eyes weren't watering from the sting of the brushing, I level my glare and force words past the lump of steel in my throat. "You think I have the luxury of caring what you useless pig bladders think of me?"

"You defined your priorities on your own," she hisses. "You took it upon yourself to fight *beasts* rather than find a family, find love. You—" Her gaze flickers to the girls behind me, and I realize their hands have stilled. Onora stands and urges them to bed, laying the littlest one between them in a pile of furs. She leads me to the far side of the hut, frowning. "No one forced you into the forest that spring-tide, brightness. You had no need to prove your worth. I wish you wouldn't have."

Hot tears still plague my eyes, though my scalp is blissfully unbothered. For a moment my voice is lost as memories of that night rise with a vengeance.

Finally, I croak, "No one stopped me." The words are hardly a whisper.

Onora cups a hand to my cheek and I squeeze my eyes shut at the touch.

Blessedly, she says no more. She guides me back to my spot at the hearth and begins to work at my hair. The tugging at my skull and the smoke in my nose return me to the familiar comfort of agony, and I succumb to it.

$\mathcal{I}$ pat at my braids as I walk to my hut; the sleek locks that now crown my head, I am certain, cannot be mine.

Though still coarser and wilder than Onora's—and a far cry from the unearthly silkiness of Dìomath's—the intricate latticework at the back of my head is more befitting of a maiden than a warrior. Unburdened of bones, bearsbane, blood, and worse, my hair feels strangely light. I don't know what to make of it.

I wonder what Dìomath will think, and without more than a spared thought for sleep I know will not come, my feet have changed course, my toes descending upon soft, moonlit earth that gives way to the detritus of Bairnhart Forest's floor. I hurry past skeletal branches, tugging my bear pelts tightly around me to ward off the chill that accompanies their hypnotic swaying, leaping over roots bursting from the soil in great loops and ridges and fallen trees swaddled under combs of feathery moss.

It is my third return to the forest this day.

I set out to kill the foul She-Bear; to liberate Hazelfeur from the plague of her spawn—and yet that is the furthest thing from my mind. I wonder at the drastic difference in my disposition: did a vengeful mania blind me when I first set out with Nathaire to slay Artio? Or is it now, under the stars' scathing watch, that I am possessed by inexplicable madness?

My hand strays from Thornfury's handle and goes again to my hair, smoothing the unknotted stalks that flow to my waist. Combed slick and tight over my scalp and held only by a twisted netting of braids around the base of my skull, the longer lengths explode in a fury of autumnal frizz over my shoulders. It's impractical, hanging so freely, and I feel as if I could shed my furs and look almost feminine—the thought stops me in my tracks mere steps away from Dìomath's hollow. I blink at my dirty feet, illuminated by a finger of supernal light poking through the misty mesh of never-fall leaves above, and my fingers pluck absently at the hairs on my forearms as I consider shedding my mantle.

The bearskin is from my first kill, the early spring day one I remember with fondness. The beast had ravaged Hazelfeur's pastures, leaving the livestock pens a bloody mess and the elders worrying for the village's hunger. Several weeks had passed since my awakening as Bearslayer, and I was consumed by a raging grief at the loss of my favorite goat, an obnoxious little thing that had only one eye and the bleat of a mating toad. While the elders held council and the men failed to reinforce the remaining livestock pens, I took up my scythe and tracked the trail of viscera to the bear's den, where I had hoped to find it sleeping. It was not asleep.

The beast took me by surprise and nearly knocked my bones from my body with its weight, then nearly skinned me whole as I struggled to discern up from down. I had little skill with Thornfury then, but managed to cleave through the bear's belly with his blade. I returned to Hazelfeur dragging its hide behind me, dizzy with blood loss, and the elders—despite their worrying—prepared a feast for my victory. They praised me as the Bear-Killing Maiden, and Èilde Malvynn made the bear's skin into a hooded mantle, held together at my sternum by a clasp of bone from the one-eyed goat, carved elegantly into the head of a rose.

The battle left me with a half-dozen pulpy scars roping across my torso from armpit to hip—I had begged Onora to do everything she could to magick them away with her ointments, but now I am glad for them. There's something sensuous in the way they wrap around me; a pattern for curious fingers to follow.

And yet still I do not want Dìomath to see them, and so I leave the furs clasped about my chest.

"Dìomath," I say as I near the hollow's opening. "Are you well?"

I hear a strange shifting, and then her voice, thick with sleep—"Rhoswen?"

Slipping into the burrow, I stammer an apology. "Ah, I didn't think...it's so late, and you need rest. I just wanted to..."

"No, please," Dìomath interrupts, holding out a slender

hand, grace embodied. Nestled into the wall of the hollow, upright and unruffled, she doesn't look as if she has been sleeping.

"Are you in pain?" I ask, again on my knees before her. I reach for the bandage around her thigh, but her hand catches my fingers, and my breath catches in my ribcage.

"No pain," she promises, her smile an undiluted drop of radiance. "I know you likely have questions, and I owe them to you."

I am dazed by her touch, my mind obscured by a milky fog. "Questions?"

"About why I am unable to leave these woods."

Artio's woods, a tinny voice reminds me. I slowly—reluctantly—pull my hand away from hers. "You said you were bound. By blood."

Dìomath nods, averting her gaze.

"These are Artio's woods," I say at the urging of the voice in my head, prompting her to elaborate.

"They are my mother's woods," she murmurs. She buries her face in her hands.

I narrow my eyes, trying to get my lips to form words, glad she can't see the contortions of my face. "Your... mother...?"

A shrill gasp escapes her. "Oh, Rhoswen!" she sobs. "I should have told you. But I feared you would despise me for it—"

"Your mother," I say again, the words falling heavy from my mouth, struggling to reconcile *mother's woods* with

Artio's woods. "These are Artio's woods, Dìomath. The bears, the wraiths...they are all hers."

Again she nods, her face still concealed by her splayed fingers. "As am I," she moans, her narrow shoulders shuddering.

I feel as if I should do something—move, or speak, or plunge Thornfury into her heart, or perhaps into mine— but I am as tethered to the ground as the whorls of roots arcing over our heads. Frozen, even in the face of Dìomath's warm glow.

"You're what?"

She finally lifts her head from her palms. The wreath of roots sits crookedly over her brow, and for a moment she bears the eerie image of a horned púca.

Then she rights it, a crowned lady once more, and says, "I am a daughter of Artio."

Nathaire has often told me I should learn to run. He knows it's hopeless; that no urging will force me to flee in the face of danger or uncertainty. Though he thinks I nurture no fear when it comes to bearslaying—though I let him believe it—it is not the truth. I am intimately acquainted with fear; with the way it turns my feet to lead; the way its claws of ice seize upon my legs; the way it doesn't touch me at all and yet paralyzes me to my very core. It is neither friend nor enemy, but a constant acquaintance, and it is because of fear that I cannot move when Dìomath confesses her heritage.

Strangely, I think again of my hair, its weightlessness palpable, the creeping ache of tiredness up my spine more noticeable now that my neck is unburdened of the knotted mass. Only a single wraith bone remains speared through the bundle of braids twisted away from my temples. The rest I nearly surrendered to Onora's hearth, but instead tucked into a pouch of bearsbane at my hip, unwilling to part with the hard-earned tokens of my victories.

Victories against Artio's children. Dìomath's kin.

"Please, don't leave," Dìomath begs when I remain rigid, wordless. "I am not...fond. Of my mother. It is by her blood that I..." Her brow wrinkles and her gaze lingers on her wounded thigh. "I am cursed, Rhoswen."

Still I do not speak, though the vise of ice begins to thaw.

Dìomath gestures at her leg. "A bear did not do this." Then she points to me—no, to Thornfury. "That did."

And then I understand, and I shake my head furiously, remembering the bright-eyed fleshbear from earlier in the day, the one that appeared from nowhere and disappeared as it came. The way Thornfury missed his mark and instead grazed the beast's leg.

"You can... You? The bear? *You* attacked me?"

Her expression does not change, but something flickers under her pained visage like movement under water's surface, a silvery flash there and then gone. "Only to defend myself. Were you not there to hunt me?"

"Not you," I spit. "Your mother."

Another flicker, and then her features smooth. Tears pearl in her eyes. "Rhoswen, please. I have no more love for her than you do, not when she has made me into...*this*."

I fall back on my haunches at the crack of her honeyed voice. Heat and ice war within me at the way she begs me. I swallow hard, pinching my fingertips, pressing the arc of my nail into the callouses, all too conscious of her eyes upon me.

"I'm sorry I hurt you," I blurt at the same time she says,

"Your hair is different."

My cheeks heat, and she laughs, and the ice melts away fully.

"The hurt didn't last," Dìomath assures me, and at my frown she sheepishly pulls aside the bloodied cloth to reveal unblemished ivory skin.

I gape. "How is this so?"

"Bear goddess blood, I suppose."

I touch her leg and it is smoother than even my unscarred skin—no trace of the gash Thornfury had inflicted but for the dried blood on her skirt.

"Onora would eat a crow," I marvel.

She nods, her smile a sacred twinkle. "She would." Her knuckle brushes my fingers, still shamefully stroking her leg, and she asks solemnly, "Do you despise me, Rhoswen?"

"Never," I say without thought, then wince at my eagerness. I clear my throat. "I am only...thinking. Are all of Artio's children like you? Are all the bears human?"

"Human," she muses, rolling her shoulders backwards. "No. And they are not her children, the bears, the wraiths. Not anymore. Just her creations. Were I her creation, perhaps she would love me as she does them."

Artio—capable of love? I find it unlikely, but am unsure the thought would alleviate Dìomath's melancholy. "And you. Why does she keep you here?"

A pause. "She worries I would slander her name."

"She does that well enough herself," I say. "She seems intent upon torturing my people. Do you know what qualms she has with Hazelfeur?"

Dìomath cocks her head to the side and opens her mouth to answer, but a noise rumbles through the ground from the darkness beyond the hollow, deep and grating, like the earth itself waking. Her face becomes a mask of fear and she leaps to her feet, gathering up her skirts and casting aside the circlet.

I stand with a frown, longing to run my thumb along her forehead to smooth away the wrinkles. "What is it?"

"I must go—*you* must go." She pushes me toward the opening. Her grasp lingers on my arm. "Will you come back?"

"Aye, enchantress." The word slips out before I can bite my tongue, but Dìomath doesn't seem to notice, so affected is she by the movement from the bowels of the burrow. I place my hand over hers. "Will you be alright?"

She bobs her head and pulls away, and I retreat above ground, my heart hammering.

As I turn to cast one last glance down the hole, I spy a swish of green skirts and a streak of sorrel feathers—no, fur—and then my enchantress, my creature of the forest, is gone.

I hurry back to Hazelfeur, doggedly twisting away from the lumbering shadows of Bairnhart, unsure, if it came to it, if I could cause a fleshbear harm, knowing what I do now.

Dìomath, daughter of Artio, ursine shifter.

Girl, spawn, bear.

Her beautiful face so marred by fear nags at me, an insufferable itch beneath my skin, and I long, again, to turn back. I long to steal Dìomath away from her hole in the ground, to take her far from Artio's lair.

When I come to my hut, warm shards of light flicker through the woven wattle and for a moment I am certain Artio has come to reckon with me. Then the ambrosial nip of goldroot loosens my nostrils and I realize it is only Nathaire.

He looks up from the bowl in his lap when I duck inside, his eyes rung with shadows. His hands slash through the air. *"Sweet stench of Aengus's toenails, Roz, where have you been?"*

"I was tending to the girl, the wounded one. In the forest."

"What was she doing in the forest?" he asks, stooping to

67

pour me a bowl of tea.

"She—lives there," I stammer, realizing it's the truth. I never hide things from Nathaire, but Dìomath's heritage makes me hesitate. "She's cursed."

His eyes rake over me, lingering on Dìomath's blood, then on my hair, his brow marred by a tiny ridge of concern. *"And Artio?"*

I shake my head, feeling suddenly cold. With a heavy sigh, I join him by the fire and greedily sip at the hot tea, letting its liquid comfort sizzle through me. "She didn't deign to show herself. I should have looked harder...I was distracted."

"A boy died," Nathaire signs, solemnly nodding.

I close my eyes, blood surging to my ears in a rush, roaring so fiercely I can scarcely hear the popping of the fire.

A boy died.

An oily shiver threads through my chest, and I laugh aloud at the way it wracks my body, earning me a quizzical look from Nathaire as he sets his bowl aside.

"Women are distracting," I explain, stirring the gold-root leaves with a finger.

He snatches the bowl from me, sun-browned skin cracking as he wrinkles his nose. *"Your hands! Gods, you are an animal sometimes."*

"Do you not think women are distracting?"

"This seems like a trap."

I shrug and draw the tip of my tongue over the sharp point of a tooth, then press the pad of my thumb to it, evoking another affronted squawk from Nathaire. He stands and goes to dump the bowls out, first tossing a soggy wad of goldroot leaves at me, which I catch and cram against the roof of my mouth as I drop onto my bed of furs. I let the essence trickle down my throat and with it comes the song of nightbirds, the dream of hidden groves, the solace of a woolen cocoon. It is not enough to put me to sleep, but it lulls me into a hazy, heavy-lidded stupor through which I watch Nathaire stoke the fire and listen to the low hum of his voice. He uses it so rarely that I am immediately captivated, drawn back centuries by its depth.

When he puts down the soot-ended stick, he begins to sign with a rhythmic flow, the speed of his movements ebbing with the rise and fall of his humming.

> "It began on a true summer night,
> I saw my dove, my love, take flight.
> lover of thorns, edges roughhewn,
> silken petals crowned with dew,
> and a promise hidden in sinful brew;
> I drank it all under a monsoon moon.
> A sin-sick dreamer, I sing for you,
> splendor clothed in bright true light,
> my dove, my love, with me take flight.
> Seasons' change peddles sweet time,
> I buy two summers to call you mine.
> This tender heart, sweet starshine,

diviner's foresight cannot be denied.

With me, my dove, our love takes flight..."

"Which of the gods is that about?" I ask him. Raised chiefly by the elders as I was—if not with a more respectful ear—Nathaire was often subjected to their warblings of the gods; grim songs of Morrigan's crows, lilting odes to Áine's beauty, throaty hymns enjoining Danu's fertility.

He shrugs, leaving the coals to simmer. *"Some say it was sung by the Dagda to a mortal lover whom he had killed for worshipping the stars instead of kissing his feet. Some say he did not kill her, but played his harp to turn back the seasons, to bring her back from the dead. They were in love."*

I sit up, my pelts tumbling down my arms. "His harp can turn back the seasons?"

"Among other marvels." Nathaire scoffs, kneading his knuckles into his sternum. *"Yet he prefers to squander its powers on magicking spirits into his craw, and the like."*

"Where is it found?" I ask.

"The spirits? In his craw."

"No, goathead," I gasp, my mind afuzz. "The *harp*. Where is the Dagda's harp?"

He stares at me, and I frown at a stray curl caught infuriatingly on his eyelashes, wisps of it waggling so near the glassy void of his iris that it's a wonder he doesn't notice. I reach out to swat it away, ignoring the quirk of his scarred eyebrow, and try to root through my goldroot-mossed thoughts.

"*You should sleep, Roz,*" Nathaire signs at last. "*Spring is upon us.*"

He slips outside, leaving me to pace the length of my hut, trying to mollify the quiet gnaw of restlessness in my legs. I mull over his words.

He played his harp to turn back the seasons.

Could the Dagda's harp turn the seasons from the tide of Artio's domain?

Could it—could *he*—be persuaded to neglect spring altogether?

I seek out Èilde Malvynn under the hawthorn tree, where I know he offers prayers before sunswake. I find him whittling, his wrinkled fingers chalked with osseous dust. I cannot make out more than a pointed face protruding from the tiny block of bone.

Èilde Malvynn looks up as I draw near and smiles, leathery bunches of brown, buttery skin creasing down his neck. He tucks the bone and his carving knife under the crisp plume of nimbus blue he wears across his chest.

"Warrior rose," he says, his voice thick and syrupy, rolling with a timbre of warmth. "Blessed springtide."

I stiffen—*a boy's death, a blessing?*—but tilt my head in a polite nod. "Apologies for disturbing you, but I come seeking wisdom."

The elder laughs and looks up at the burgeoning spires of thorned branches. "From the tender-hearts' tree, or from me?"

"Whichever of you knows of the Dagda's lore."

"I've never known you to pay much mind to the gods," Èilde Malvynn says with a tilt of his head.

"The Dagda isn't much of a god anymore from what I hear."

If the elder thinks me a heretic, he doesn't show it, only grunts. "Aye, he has little affinity for godliness. But he does what we ask of him, and we owe him thanks. What is it you wish to know?"

Sucking on my tongue, I look down. The early suns-wake light greases the freckles on my arms and illuminates a wisp-thin hair, making it glint. I pinch it between the nubs of my fingernails and yank it out.

"The Dagda's harp," I venture. "Its mystical properties, and...its whereabouts."

"Ah," he says. "The legendary Ràithne. Season's harbinger. Truthfully I know very little, only rumors of her prowess. Her ability turned the tides of war in the favor of Dagda's people in an age long past, but I know not how. It may be only myth."

"Do you believe it to be myth?"

Malvynn's lips thin in a suppressed smile. "Would my belief change the reality of it? I cannot speak for its existence, but when I listen very closely at the dawn of a new season, I hear something I cannot explain."

"The harp?" I press.

"Perhaps. It is a sound..." His eyes, the dark umber of tulsi berries, mist over. "Unfathomable. A godly thing, aye, but its source? I am not sure the god of the wild could, himself, track it. It may be Ràithne's sweet song, it may be the shift of the stars, who am I to say?"

I bite back a sickening swell of frustration. I knew it was unlikely the elders would be of much use, but I refused to consult the púca without trying. "Èilde Malvynn, I also wished to ask of Hazelfeur's history with Artio."

"History with Artio? We have no history with Artio. She has never emerged from her realm in Bairnhart, not in my lifetime." His jaw quivers as he chews the husk of a fulcress bulb. "Aye, you know this better than anyone."

"There must be a reason for her wrath," I insist, pinching my fingertips.

Onetwothree.

I could be hunting Artio.

Onetwothree.

I could be with Dìomath.

"The gods are as full of reason as they are of mortality," Malvynn says. "Their existence does not center on us so much as it does on demonstrating their magnificence. They are less concerned with notions of purpose than you are, dear Bearslayer."

nsatisfied with Èilde Malvynn's wealth of knowledge, I venture beyond the village, over a low rock wall crumbling with age and blanketed by creeping thyme and fronds of maidenhair. Past the wall, unbothered by our little village, the dip and sway of bowed fields and steep rockfaces rise toward the horizon, deliberately stretching to kiss the powdered morning sky, which bears down around me, an ambient ether that coaxes easy breaths from my lungs. The sun, ripe above the scrublands, does not yet burn with the heat of high spring.

Sprays of prairie clover tickle my ankles as I walk, their coned purple heads bobbing politely in my wake as I make my way carefully around the bestrewn piskie burrows. Though the openings are spiderwebbed, the tiny beasties inside likely just rousing from their winter sleep, I still avoid them. Many equinoxes past, contesting for our first hunt, Nathaire and I dashed through these fields in pursuit of a fat hare. Our reckless footfalls disturbed the slumbering piskies and they emerged, naked and beautiful, and trapped us in the fields for two days, knotting our hair as we slept and stealing threads from our clothes to wrap around themselves. One particularly angry creature nipped off the tip of Nathaire's little toe.

Had we caught the hare, it might have been a fond memory.

I sneak through the clover and past the swells of heather until I come upon the patch of hope roses where, as a babe, I opened my eyes for the first time—where an elder found me swaddled in a bed of glossy, toothed leaves and sprays of frilled ivory and pale yellow.

As I always do when visiting my cradle, I lay in the cluster of roses, sprawling for a moment amongst the young blooms, breathing in their sweet-citrus perfume, the sky framed by ruffles of blushing aureate petals.

Though the roses would make a beautiful deathbed, they make a lousy mother.

A slick shard of agitation stabs behind my eyes, and I clamber out of the shrubbery. With Thornfury's scythe, I cut through a single stalk, shearing off a rose head. An offering for the púca.

Before turning away, I contemplate the hope roses, then shear off a whole bundle of heads, piling them against my breast. A gift for my enchantress.

I gather bunches of heather and tufts of maidenhair as I return to the village, squatting longer each time to search for the jewels of the crop. Then I swallow the bitter anxiety that rises and rises ever toward my throat and march up to the púca's temple.

Spring must be put to rest—for Hazelfeur's well-being; for Dìomath's freedom.

I place the rose at the foot of the temple.

"A rose from the warrior rose," says a wolfish púca, the flower suspended from its jagged talons before I've even straightened my spine. It brings the petals to its snout, then crushes them between stained fangs. "Gratitudes."

Forcing myself to meet the sprite's predatory gaze, I clear my throat to speak. "Thornfury's pleasure. But I—I wish to... I beg your wisdom."

"Mmm." The púca makes a grating, throaty sound. "*Beg.* You need not beg when you have so much to offer, Bear-slayer."

My nerves pulse in my fingertips. I should have known I would not be walking away from this temple without a debt weighing my shoulders. A rose? Hardly a thing of value.

"I will be beholden to you," I murmur, trying to keep the loathing out of my voice.

The púca offers a horrible smile, its snarling visage furling under the inverted arch of its horns. "So you will."

"I seek knowledge of the Dagda and his harp."

"Knowledge? Or vengeance?"

I dig my thumbnail into my fingertips: *onetwothree, onetwothree, onetwothree.* "All I wish to know is its location."

"And why, pray tell, do you assume we know such things?" Saliva glistens in the fleshy folds beneath its chin.

"Do your kind not have loyalties to the gods?"

"It would hardly serve us to pledge to the gods."

I hesitate. "One god, then?"

Another wicked smile splits its snout like a half-moon. "Clever Bearslayer."

"If you don't know of the harp's whereabouts, I owe you no debt," I say with a scowl. "All I ask is a direction. You needn't even speak."

"Were it so simple."

I wipe my palms on my pelts, wishing again that I could shake sense into the ancestors who made the Pact with these infuriating creatures, and roll my head back to loosen the ever-taut muscles in my neck. I say nothing.

"The Dagda is not our patron," the púca drawls, a flicker of annoyance in the twitch of its ears, "and indeed, we have little regard for him—I reckon a blind goose could better strum the lovely Ràithne than he..."

"So you don't know where the harp is?" I growl, prepared to revoke my debt.

"I do not have a direction."

Onetwothreeonetwothree—

"But I know the path that will lead you," it says finally, seemingly pleased at my impatience, or perhaps at the desperation that anchors me. "The tide which commands man."

I can hardly keep my hands from knotting into my hair, so frayed is my composure. I must have been standing here like a fool for hours now, humoring the púca in its little game. My frustration swells in my throat; I wave my hand, gesturing for it to continue.

The púca again bristles at my silence, but speaks nevertheless. "The emotions of man will lead you to Ràithne. Sorrow and mirth, peace and fear. This is the trail she leaves—such is her power over your kind; such sway has her springtide song."

"She affects the minds of men?"

"You seem surprised. Is that not the feminine design?"

I wouldn't know, I think, but I don't enlighten the sprite of my womanly ignorance. "I should look for signs of... what, madness, then?" I ask. "How am I to know who her song has touched?"

"Mm," it hums, dragging a claw across its teeth. "Perhaps to the north, warrior rose."

And then it's gone.

"*Y*ou have no bearsbane," Nathaire signs, touching the braids tucked behind my ears, frowning at them.

I chew on my lip, uncertain if I should pretend it wasn't intentional. Batting his hand away, I worry my fingers over my hair, already frizzed with tangles at which Onora would shake her head.

"It's never done much for keeping the bears away, has it?" I say, but to appease him I pause from gathering supplies to find a string of dried bearsbane and tie it around my neck.

As I left the púca's temple, Nathaire had silently fallen into stride with me. At his knowing look, I had shared with him my intent to find the Dagda's harp. He didn't speak as we slipped back to my hut, and still I await his protests, his demands to accompany me.

They don't come.

"You will stay here in my stead," I say, oiling a sharpening stone to hone Thornfury's blade. The stone wails against the metal, an awful resonance of the flurry in my bones. "Expect an attack soon—a day has passed since the last."

"*Since a boy died,*" Nathaire signs with careful fingers. "*I know.*"

"Don't leave the village if you can help it. Don't leave them without protection, Natty, they can't be left—"

"*Tell it to the bees, Roz. I know what to do.*"

I pause at the sudden snap of his hands, taking him in. He stands, unmoving, his dark gaze cast toward the ground.

"Nathaire?" I ask, abandoning Thornfury to reach for him.

He pulls back, his brow a harsh ridge. "*What changed?*"

Taken aback, a response failing to tumble from my tongue, I gape dumbly.

"*You have never sought a solution before. You have never—*" He stops, shaking his head. "*You insist on protecting Hazelfeur. On being Bearslayer. What changed?*"

My hand goes to the bear claw netted in pale hair resting against my sternum. "A boy *died*—"

"*Boys have died before,*" he signs, his fingers snarling, his eyes finally flashing to meet mine, uncharacteristically ablaze, "*and still you insist your protection is enough. And now? What has changed, Rhoswen?*"

Heat pulses behind my eyes, in my ears, under my tongue. "I've never thought to seek other solutions. But things have only gotten worse, Nathaire, every year worse."

"*You went to hunt Artio.*" Nathaire stops; his jaw pulses as his tongues push against the inside of his cheek, and I know he's holding back accusations—accusations which are not unfounded. My shame simmers hot. "*And since then you have not been present, and now you want to steal from the Dagda, and you were not—"* His forehead pinches. *"You were not wearing bearsbane."*

"The girl in the forest," I blurt, and it sounds like a poor excuse, but it is the truth. For Dìomath, I forsook protection. For Dìomath, all.

Nathaire does not seem surprised. He waits for me to go on.

"She's...sensitive," I say haltingly, unwilling to reveal the secrets my enchantress entrusted to me, if for no other reason than to call them mine. "To green things."

He chalks out a laugh, shakes his head, and dips his fingers into the pouch at his hip, a feathered sprig of goldroot disappearing into his mouth. For a long moment, eyes glazed, he chews on the leaf. Then he asks, *"Do you care for her?"*

Care for, bewitched by, in awe of.

"I am..." I close my eyes, searching for words that won't betray the soft, wondrous madness blooming within me, "curious of her soul."

Again Nathaire laughs, this time with real humor at my sentimentality. His hands move with their characteristic softness. *"Oh, Roz."*

Though he finally comes nearer, squeezes my shoulder, and presses his lips to my forehead, there's a rigidity about him I've not experienced before.

"I could watch out for her while you are away, if she came to the village," he offers.

"She can't," I say, quickly drawing away from him and returning to Thornfury's blade.

His eyebrow snakes toward his hairline. *"Green things, I presume?"*

I scowl at him and reply with a rude gesture. As he moves away to make tea, I wonder at my indistinct reflection in the scythe's metal.

Were the deaths of past springs my doing?

With assurances from Nathaire that Hazelfeur will not fall to ruin in my absence and streaks of Onora's protective paints on my face and arms, I depart the village. I take the púca's recommendation to head north, though it's not as if there are many other options. The scrublands of Hazelfeur extend in every direction, but to the east and the south the fields give way to sand and sea, and to the west are the depthless forests of Bairnhart. To the north, groves of hazel trees crawl into the knolls and foothills that skirt burgeoning mountains, the gilded peaks of which boldly stab the sky's underbelly.

Nathaire calls them the *Palace of the Bees*. I've never thought much about the mountains, nor anything beyond Hazelfeur, only wondered if bees would be better than bears.

Judging by how few of my worries the bees have actually unburdened me of, I remain uncertain.

Though I know I should make haste toward the mountains to search for the Dagda's harp, I find myself cutting across the fields, a knotting of whispers under my ribcage as I shear toward Bairnhart Forest; toward the hole in the ground where fate smiled upon me.

The woods seem almost to welcome me, even the fallen crush of yesteryear shimmering merrily under a melting dew, the path on which my feet fly bright and clear. I fuse the dark distortions of my anxieties into a tight lump and banish them to a dusty region of my mind, ignoring the jagged fragments that splinter off and prod with distress at the frothing thoughts of viridescent eyes and a voice like rain.

As I near Dìomath's hollow, I open my mouth, but movement beyond the clearing catches my eye and her name dies on my lips. The roses and heather and maidenhair I gathered from the scrublands tumble from my arms, replaced by the familiar weight of Thornfury's chain hanging slack between its grip and the handle of his blade.

A fleshbear rises from all fours, its front paws hovering, uncertain, unthreatening.

By the time I comprehend the wariness and notice the softness of its gaze, the branches looped around its ears, instinct has already flung Thornfury's scythe from my hand, and I watch the steel carve across the clearing.

A nebulous gasp of horror rips through me and I snap the chain—the outer curve of the blade jerks away from the fleshbear, a mere breath away from its chest, and ricochets back to me. Thornfury whines through the air, angry at being denied bear blood, and my muscles scream in similar protest as I drop my weapon and stand before the fleshbear empty-handed.

"Dìomath," I murmur, my voice tight with turmoil, dazed by this unnatural feeling of intentional inaction; this encounter that renders me something other than Bearslayer.

I feel unsteady as I meet the bear's eyes—*her* eyes, the same but for the fur surrounding them—and only unsteadier as the bear suddenly becomes a woman, the two forms so irreconcilable that I feel a piskie must have pulled a veil over my eyes to muddle reality.

But which is the reality—the girl or the bear?

"Rhoswen?" Dìomath's concern pierces my haze of confusion. I notice a diaphanous shimmer to her dress, some unassuming magic preserving her modesty during the shifting. "You look ill."

"You're a bear," I say, at first an accusation and then an uncertainty. I shake my head and scratch my cheek, cursing when I smear Onora's intricate brightness, frowning at the wetness of it on my fingertips. It shimmers scarlet and gold in the sunlight, smells of sweetroot and clay. My mind goes blank as I scrutinize it—this clear, understandable substance. It is just paint, and nothing else.

I blink and wipe my hand on my trousers, then return my gaze to Dìomath, who has moved closer but lingers several yards away, undoubtedly thinking me mad. Distress clouds the sharp features of her face.

"I'm sorry," I stammer, still steadfastly scrubbing paint from my palm. "I know you're a bear, you know, you...I just..." I gesture vaguely, shake my head again, and drop both hands to my sides. "I brought you flowers."

A wicked glint shadows her face, cruel as a crow's caw, and then is gone—a trick of the light?—and in its place a pearly, childish glow of delight. Her eyes, those vivid secrets, go to the hope roses scattered at my feet. "They're beautiful."

I stoop to pick them up. She kneels to help me, and when her knuckle brushes mine I suck in my breath, then seize her hand, feeling along her fingers.

Fingers, not claws.

Girl, not bear.

"I didn't mean to startle you," Dìomath says, tangling her fingers with mine. "It's safer for me to maintain the form my mother prefers."

The frost in my blood abates at her touch, and I wonder if I've ever been so warm before. This, I feel, is what it is to be a raindrop permeated by sunlight, bewitched without choice by a sacred warmth.

Realizing the intensity of my silence, I swallow hard, my palm slick against hers, and say, "You have large hands."

Dìomath's mouth drops open and she tragically draws her hand away, but there's humor in the tilt of her head. "What?"

"I didn't—it wasn't meant as an insult," I splutter. I hold my hands up in explanation. "I have large hands, see? Larger than yours. My people have such small hands, I've always felt like a big-boned beast among them. Not that you're big-boned! Your bones seem...lovely. Danu's tits, I swear I've not had a drop of strong waters, Dìomath."

She laughs, to my immense relief, and presses her palm to mine, contemplating our hands, the corners of her eyes crinkled. "I suppose you're right." Her forefinger curls, tickling the shiny pink skin roped between my fore and middle finger. "Though your hands tell more stories than mine, don't they?"

My skin thrills under her gauzy touch. "They're not stories you want to hear," I whisper.

Dìomath's hooded eyes meet mine, conveying some unfamiliar language, trapping me like a fowl under one of Nathaire's arrows. She drags her hand down, trailing feather touches along the crescent-moon scar on the pad of my thumb, across the long-faded cluster curling around my wrist.

"Piskie bites," I say of the speckled scar, my voice quavering. "Damned beasties chewed off a gauntlet I spent long moons crafting. I had carved it prettily—and they like pretty things."

"Must be why they bit you," Dìomath teases, her voice bold but her eyes suddenly shy.

Her meaning dawns on me with a flood of heat to my cheeks. *Bless you, Onora,* I think, hoping my blush is concealed beneath the paint. I fumble with the stem of a hope rose, shaking my head vehemently as I weave it into her circlet of twigs. "I'm not pretty. Not like you."

"Is that why you changed your hair?" she asks, offering a sprig of heather and bowing her head so I can more easily work it into the withies.

I hesitate. "I...I don't know. I've never cared much about my hair."

Dìomath lifts her head. Her face is as bright and intense as late sunsleep, and my breath hitches as she reaches around me, her fingers going to the base of my skull, so close I can feel her breath against my throat. I feel my hair spring free of Onora's tidy braids, heavy locks of it falling forward in a wild veil, surrounding my vision in a haze of auburn. I'm breathless as Dìomath pushes her hands through it, her eyes still speaking that phantasmal, secret language—one of virgin shadows brought to light; of sprawling meadows aglow with mizzle; of the delicate silk of a spiderweb humming soundlessly; of something depthless and unbound and unafraid.

When she kisses me, I feel neither heat nor ice nor the persistent gnaw of my nerves. I feel only a soft rush, starlight surging through my veins, a burgeoning bliss settling like a second skin as we break apart with gentle gasps.

We laugh, each of us stealing the other's breath, a wordless exchange of ambrosial intangibility, together in a cocoon of suspended disbelief.

iomath is radiant in her crown, now adorned with bells of muted mauve and pale yellow and a green that is greyed by the luster of her eyes. She strikes me as a goddess, and though I have not forgotten that isn't far from the truth, I am certain no deity is as beautiful as she.

Dìomath, unlike her mother, is worthy of revere.

Having persuaded me to stay with her a while longer, my enchantress leads me through Bairnhart Forest. We walk hand in hand, Bearslayer and She-Bear's daughter, our irreconcilable realities neglected for a time, cast off in favor of simplicity—of savoring our unlived girlhoods.

I abandon my pelts, already long having forsaken the swathe of bearsbane I wore to appease Nathaire, worried Dìomath would take offense or realize the implications of our attraction. Though she swore she harbored no love for her kin, bear is still in her blood—the same blood that weighs, suddenly heavy, on my conscience.

At a thawed stream, Dìomath sheds her dress and plunges into the water up to her waist with a shriek of exhilaration, then immediately leaps back to the bank, breathless, mischief in the glint of her eyes.

"Go on," she says to me, knocking her elbow against mine, the flesh of her collarbone prickled with chill. "It's not cold, I swear it."

I tweak her trembling chin, raising a doubtful brow. "Is it not? You're certain?"

She nods, the solemnity of her eyes a stark contrast to the youthful pout of her lips as she tries to keep her teeth from chattering. "Not in the slightest."

"Are you trying to say I need a bath?" I ask, stripping down to my undertunic. Gooseflesh erupts where Dìomath's gaze lingers on my bare skin, having nothing to do with the cold, and fire sears along my exposed scars. "Crows, you're as bad as Onora."

I toe the water's edge, disrupting the wavering image of my unkempt hair and sun-mottled face. Rapturous clarity descends, the iciness spearing through my discomfort, and before wading deeper I spin around, snatching Dìomath by the arms and towing her into the depths with me. There's a moment of deafening silence as her face marbles, cold as the river, and then she's laughing, jeweled cries falling upon my ears as she clings to me. Our hair mingles, silvered by the water, and hope roses fallen from her head swirl in the ripples around us before floating downstream, treasures of the earth borne on currents toward uncertain destinies. I watch them before they disappear, wishing I, too, could succumb to the river's pull.

A shifting of the goat willows and alder trees on the

opposite bank sends a plume of ice scorching down my spine and I jerk Dìomath behind me, pressing my back to her, pushing toward the shore where Thornfury lays abandoned.

But Dìomath does not move, and I shiver as her palm anchors on my hip. "It is not my brethren, Rhoswen," she murmurs, her lips grazing my shoulder. The tension of my muscles softens and melts under her breath. "Look."

The great crooked branches of the river alders sweep reverently toward the water, their catkins and infant leaves drooping low over its surface, the pockmarked pillars of their trunks bowing uncomfortably close to snapping. The goat willows, already forlorn in posture, bend further over the river, also seeming to bow.

Never have the hazel trees bowed to Hazelfeur's elders —nor to the púca. Older than time, lifegiving deities themselves, the treefolk bow only to the gods who allow them dominion over their land.

And to Dìomath, it would seem.

"Come," my enchantress urges quietly. "The willows and alders are prone to bickering over the better spots to tease the asrai when they come out at moonswake. They think I don't know of their flirtations, or their fighting, but they're quite noisy. I spy on them sometimes."

Her last words take on a tone of wishful melancholy and as we wade back to our discarded garments on the shore I wonder if she shares the same sentiments of loneliness as I.

"Asrai?" I question, glancing over my shoulder to see

the alders straighten their spines and bristle as if to rid themselves of the disgrace of obeisance. "River folk?"

Dìomath nods. "Nightfaring water spirits. Shy faeries; they speak only to the trees. It's a shame they don't stay long in Bairnhart—they migrate to colder waters after springtide. My—my mother's spawn mistake them for fish." A small smile perks her paled lips.

"I'm not familiar with water spirits," I say, mostly to distract myself from the lingering blaze of desire emanating from where Dìomath gripped my hip. "There's a lake near my village, but the elders claimed it for their bathing. I think our well was once home to a nymph, but some piskies trapped a feral badger at the bottom with it and they didn't get along. The badger may still be down there, come to think of it. The well does make strange noises..."

I trail off, realizing Dìomath now stands fully clothed. I hasten into my trousers and tunic. "Dìomath, I should...I'll be leaving for a time. I'm going in search of the Dagda's harp. It is my intent not only to liberate Hazelfeur from Artio's wrath, but to free you from her captivity as well."

That strange liquid visage ripples under her expression, coloring her with a perversity of innocence, the light's inclination to play mischief on her face casting her in a shroud of dark allure that I find less becoming of an enchantress and more befitting of my immortal nemesis. At the creeping thought, a shiver ices the blissful heat I've harbored since our kiss, but then it's passed and Dìomath brushes her fingers against my wrist, her charming softness restored.

Artio must be playing tricks on me.

"Rhoswen, I cannot ask you to bear such a burden for me." Her brow pinches. "The Dagda is a conniving bastard. He bears no mercy nor love in his heart. He seduces women, tricks them, rapes them. Ràithne is his means of fooling mortals into thoughts that are not their own. He will not easily surrender her."

I sink my teeth into the fleshy inside of my cheek, let the salted anxiety wash over my tongue and down my throat, pushing it to the depths of my gut. "Aye," I croak, my fingers numb and limp in her grip. "But I have exhausted all other means of defending my people, and I can't stomach the thought of you here alone with those beasts. I must end Artio's reign."

"You are a brave creature, my big-boned warrior." A residue of concern remains in the tightness of her jaw, but her eyes twinkle and my big bones turn to water.

"How I wish I could stay here," I whisper.

$\mathcal{L}$eading me away from the river, Dìomath asks if I trust her and, though I am admittedly entranced with the way her still-wet hair clings to the arch of her back, I say yes.

"You mustn't draw your weapon," she tells me, pointedly wrinkling her nose at Thornfury.

At that I hesitate, already feeling the itch of second nature tempting my hand to Thornfury's grip, but I resist the urge and nod my promise.

She brings us to a shadowed glade, the trees whispering around us, quaking even in the windless still—perhaps gossiping about the preternatural pairing of Bearslayer and She-Bear's daughter.

Dropping my hand and cocking her head as if listening, Dìomath speaks, but they are not words my ears can translate. Roiling and guttural, I'm not certain they're words at all, but coming from her lips they don't frighten me.

What frightens me is the bear that lumbers from the swarthy pall beyond the glade.

Despite my promise, my hand snaps to my hip, fingers alighting upon soft leather. Dìomath shoots me a burning look over her shoulder, and I stay my hand, but my heart thuds a frenzied beat against my ribcage.

The fleshbear approaches Dìomath, the twin peaks of its shoulder blades rolling gracefully forward until it stops and settles its backside into the composting leafmould with a heavy *thump*. It sits and waits.

"Dìomath...?" I say uncertainly, my fingernail picking at shreds of leather peeling from Thornfury's handle.

"Éamon is mild mannered," she says, a simple statement for what is far from a simple situation. "He is young, so he is still impressionable. His loyalties are to those who provide him food and warmth—" she grins, reaching for the bear's rump "—and bum rubs."

Spring-freshened fronds tremble in my periphery, but I am unmoving, failing to understand what the bear's arse itches have to do with me.

"He can go with you," Dìomath says.

"No."

"He won't hurt you. I can ensure it, Rhoswen. He is a born protector."

Suspended in the spellbinding amber of her gaze, I pin my tongue under the sharp point of my eyetooth.

I look to the cub. Its muzzle tilts skyward, sniffing curiously, no doubt mistaking Dìomath's sweet fragrance for that of ripened fruits and honeysuckle and the son-before-the-father flowers that grow dense at the forest's edge. I can't determine if its dark eyes are intelligent or hungry.

Finally, I let my hand drop from Thornfury. Though the

wrongness of it edges red around my vision, I nod to Dìomath.

"With your word, I'll suffer the beast's company. I only wish to know—are the bum rubs essential to my well-being?"

Walking alongside the fleshbear—Éamon, though I'm reluctant to refer to him as such even in the confines of my mind—I find it difficult to breathe, unable to lose myself in the passing nature, a tempest of thirst-provoking unease unfurling in my chest. Even thoughts of my enchantress's sweet farewell fail to lift the oppressive cloak of overwhelm from my shoulders.

The memory of her words does, however, inspire lightness in my feet.

"Come back to me, my rose."

My fingertips are raw by sunsleep, the whorls of their prints interrupted by crescents of broken skin from my anxious pinching.

I've made good progress across the scrublands and must crane my neck now to see the peaks of the Bees' Palace rising into the milky twilight, though I see no signs of firelight or civilization. As I settle into a copse of budding hazel trees, watching Éamon root through the low foliage, I wonder: is the Dagda alone up there with his harp, sipping an imbibing nectar even by darkness? The tales of the Dagda told of a whole people—golden-haired, crystal-eyed demideities with whom he shared an eternal feast of glazed meats and succulent fruits plucked from the heavens, all afloat in a river of glimmering wine.

"Crows," I mumble, my tongue suddenly slick with saliva. I sift through the dried meats and berries I packed, none of which sound as enticing as the fare of the gods. My fingers brush leather at the bottom of the goatskin sack and I frown, withdrawing a worn pouch crudely carved with a coiled serpent.

Nathaire's goldroot. My soothing thing.

I crush my nose to the pouch, breathing deeply, smiling into the spirals of the serpent's tail. I shake a few gossamer leaves into my palm and slip them beneath my tongue.

As the sun renounces its last rays from the earth, the warrens empty and long-legged hares erupt from their burrows to streak through the dusk. My limbs soon loosen, and I become as the wind, flowing with a sweet serenity and a strong sense of assuredness I only experience when goldroot glides through my veins.

I survey the grove and find the mass of fur the color of seasoned hazelnuts; Éamon plods quietly through a tufted patch of white clover.

"Aye, bear!" I call. "Do you speak?"

Éamon dips his snout into the clover and ignores my shout.

"Spudheaded oaf," I mutter. I let my head fall back against the caressing branches of the hazel tree I sit in front of, peering up at the jagged mosaic its limbs cast against the forlorn blue-grey of night.

"Will you bow to me, tree?" I ask.

The tree hesitates, then obliges, and I scramble away as the spires of its branches rake down my body. It bends, rosy catkins rattling, until it's nearly prostrated before me.

I stare, openmouthed. I hadn't truly expected the tree to bow.

Determining it must be a delusion borne of the soupy fog of my thoughts, I spit out the goldroot and move away from the hazel tree, shooting it a wary glance. When it remains bowed, I wonder if it's a piskie trick. Or perhaps I'm just going mad.

I deign to ignore the tree altogether and scrub away a small circle of brush for a fire, staying clear of Éamon as I gather kindling. He seems just as keen on disregarding me, but I've no wish to inspire his interest in my existence.

Then I unsheathe Thornfury to strike my fireflint and I'm instantly aware of the bear's attention homing in on me—on the scythe that has drank countless of his brethren's blood.

Did Dìomath warn him of my blade?

"I'm only using it to start a fire," I explain uselessly, gesturing to the ground.

The bear glares.

I try to slow my breathing. "Look." I crouch and shake off my pelts despite the chill, making myself small. Holding Thornfury close to the dirt, I strike the fireflint against his steel and pray the sparks take quickly to the long stalks of grass and nettles. The kindling flares on the third strike and I lash Thornfury to my belt, leaning over the flame to coax its growth, only daring a look at Éamon when the blaze takes to the stripped buckthorn branches.

The bear has resumed his foraging in the shrubbery and I gasp in relief, bundling my furs around me so Thornfury is out of sight.

Éamon soon emerges from the bushes and ambles toward the fire, a brush rabbit limp in his maw, his beard dripping crimson. He drops it on the ground an arm's breadth away and then tromps back to the clover patch. Moments later, a rabbit's squeal pierces the air, and Éamon sets his teeth to tearing the creature's meat from its skin with frightening intensity.

I look at the first rabbit, dead aside my knee. Then I look again to Éamon. "Is this for me?" I ask.

Though I don't expect an answer, Éamon drags his muzzle from the gore of his meal and meets my gaze. The lazy roll of his eyes conveys his annoyance.

I snatch up the rabbit without looking at it, and when the bear resumes his feasting I turn my back to him, hunching over to skin the rabbit with Thornfury out of view, wondering what will it took for Éamon to provide sustenance for the slayer of his kin.

As it is wont to do, sleep evades me even in high moonswake. I stare through the dwindling flames at Éamon, who slumbers under the bush-spined crest of a foothill, his snores like thunder rolling across the scrublands.

I think of many things, each thought heavy but fleeting, the wisps of them worming in and out of my head—harps and gods and snakes, bears and roses and bowing trees.

Onora's glass beads clicking together, Nathaire's fingers spinning a song, Dìomath's lips kissing away my anxieties.

And Artio, faceless and looming, clawed hands reaching for Hazelfeur as the púca laugh and laugh and laugh.

Éamon rouses from sleep before sunswake. With the sky glowing at the earth's edge, the light's reach a murky copper finger creeping across the mountains, we set off wordlessly toward the foothills.

I glance back at the hazel tree to find it still bowed toward me, reverent, unmoving. I incline my head in return, though I'm still convinced of piskie mischief, or perhaps of Ràithne's effects—I know not how far her magic reaches, but her touch on my sanity seems more plausible than the trees having any respect for me, a lowly bear-killing maiden born to a bed of roses.

The foothills melt into the steeper slopes of the mountain. At some point during our gradual ascent toward the Palace of the Bees, I slip on an outcropping of unstable rocks, but before I can fall Éamon wedges his nose under my armpit and, with an agitated huff, shoves me to safety.

As if his nose had been white-hot, I jerk away from the bear.

"Don't *do* that, beast," I snap, sheathing my fingers into fists before I can reach for Thornfury. Familiar heat burns behind my eyes and I hiss, clamping my mouth shut though I intended to curse Éamon halfway back to his demon mother's womb.

Then I find myself on the ground, stones jutting into my stomach.

My head throbs from clenching my jaw during the climb, light squirming in my vision, and my skin feels too tight, too itchy, too warm.

I scratch at my chest, knead my knuckles against my eyes.

I realize I'm not breathing—I can't, I won't.

The air is too heavy, too sticky, too sharp.

I roll to my back, scraping off my furs, wishing I could scrape my skin off with them.

I hear a tortured animal's keening and realize distantly that it's me, sobbing for breath, my lungs stuttering wildly. It feels like a fist of broken glass in my breast tightening, tightening, tightening, and simultaneously like a beehive broken open in my skull, the buzzing growing louder, louder, louder, all of it conspiring with oblivion to end me.

It is the numbness of my lips that jars me from the panic. I dimly comprehend what it means—*air, air, air*—and know what will happen if I don't calm myself.

I will lose consciousness.

And with the spawn of my sworn enemy lurking mere yards away...

With some difficulty, I relax my shoulders, my jaw, my hips, all the places aching with tension, and steady the seizing of my ribcage.

Tell it to the bees, Roz, I imagine Nathaire signing.

"I hope the crows eat you feckers," I tell the bees in my head, and the piercing buzz in my ears abates.

I stay sprawled on my back, feeling returning to my lips and the tips of my fingers with each deep breath I take, tears and perspiration cooling on my face.

Though my body is as limp and soft as peeled fruit, heavied by exhaustion, I spring instantly to my feet at the suddenly overpowering stench of bear, too like that of Artio's lair and much too near.

No more than a leap away, Éamon sits and stares un-blinkingly at me.

"Stop it," I say with what I hope is a convincing scowl.

When he blinks, slowly and stupidly, a belt of laughter escapes me. It's a horrible, bald sound, wettened by snot, a ragged slash through the thin air enveloping me. It's fol-lowed by another bark of it, and another, and then I'm hollowed out by baseless laughter entirely.

"Stupid dumb bearspawn!" I howl, still struggling for breath. "Don't you know delirium when you see it?"

orrow, mirth, peace, fear. Ràithne's effect on man— on me—though apparently not on bears. Éamon seems to hold a curious sort of disdain for my show of emotion, the vacant orbs of his eyes having never moved from me throughout my hysterical spells.

My moment of panic was nothing I've not experienced before, but I want to believe the harp's magic aided my insanity. Now, sitting before a fire with an aching belly and swollen eyes, I fear I may burst into tears at any moment under *sorrow's* affectation.

Chewing absently on a wad of goldroot, I imagine myself creeping toward the celestial harp upon its pedestal, slipping through a hall of jeweled pillars only to shatter the silence with unbidden wails and alert the Dagda to my treachery.

I shiver, peering through smoke into the dense trees, the naked spears blurring into a singular mass—a wall of darkness that seems to inch nearer. Do they approach for my protection, or to devour me?

I blink furiously, but the goldroot weighs in my eyelids,

the anxiety of the day clinging to my bones almost comfortably, softening the descent into a dreamless sleep.

The earth's roiling wakes me.

Above, the silver scythe of the moon tumbles back and forth across a net of stars.

Dizzied by the movement and my body's swaying, I jolt forward. Coarse fur stabs my thighs through my threadbare trousers, but before confusion can dare dawn I'm slipping sideways and crashing face first to the ground.

"Danu's *tits*," I gasp, spitting moss and soil as I stagger to my feet.

When I look up, I see a dozen men, all of them fair-skinned and red-bearded and substantially unclothed, and—startling but less concerning—a giant saddled boar.

Three of the men have trapped Éamon in an absurd tangle of thick rope, and judging by the heavy panting and skewed loincloths, it is clear he put up a fight.

With the realization that we are far from where I fell asleep, and my supposed protection indisposed, I draw Thornfury out, relishing the pricks of peeling leather against my palm; the palpable chill of his fury.

The men only watch me, eyes moving in eerie synchronicity. They appear unarmed, but the beasts I'm acquainted with slaying have never borne weapons—they only have more fur.

"Ah..." I look between them, but they all seem nearly identical, and none step forward to speak. "Who are you? Where were you taking me?" I ask, and then, "Why aren't you wearing any clothes?"

The boar snorts.

"Did it just laugh?"

Still, none of the men answer, but finally they exchange glances amongst themselves.

I scrape my eyetooth along my tongue, impatient. "Do you know of the Dagda?"

One nods. "Aye."

"So you do speak," I mutter. "Why did you take me from my fire? And I *must* know—*did* the pig laugh?"

"She's Da's," another man replies, smacking the boar's flank decisively.

My fingers squeeze a needled rhythm against Thornfury's grip. "Crows, you're a helpful lot. Is this the Dagda's domain?"

A third man, identifiable from the others only by a grotesquely snarled left hand, nods. "Da."

"He enjoys adventurers," adds another.

"We've naught seen company in some time," says a fifth—or perhaps it's the same one as before; I'm too overwhelmed by the sheer amount of beard and boar to register further peculiarities.

And though I'm neither adventurer nor particularly pleasant company, I sketch a small bow to the strange throng of men. "You needn't have taken me in my sleep, then. I'm a willing company. Will you take me to him?"

Copper manes bob in assent and several fingers point to the boar, who has been lazily chewing on one of the men's loincloths.

"No." I shake my head, swatting away frizzed tangles of hair that fall into my eyes, still unbound by my enchantress's hand. "I can walk."

A dozen gazes sweep to the jagged tears in the knees of my britches, bloodied brown from my clumsy climb up the mountain's slopes.

"But you're a lady," one of the men remarks plainly.

"I've never seen a lady ride a boar," I retort.

The man shrugs, and the boar rolls her eyes with a haughtiness befitting of Onora before lumbering off, the bristled crest of fur along her spine sharpened by wet starlight. She dwarfs even the boulders peppering the rise ahead, so large that when one of the redheaded oafs clambers onto her saddle, he looks like little more than a seed sprouting from her back. Dragged along in the net of rope behind her, even Éamon looks small in comparison.

As I follow, clutching the claw at my neck, I imagine the boar's mighty hoof falling upon Éamon's skull, crushing it as if it were made of dry clay. She could crush them all, Hazelfeur's blight-beasts, crush them to dust and steal away the bears' eyes for her master, enough of them to bring bees swarming the Dagda's palace.

I could offer him that—enough honey to drown in, for his boar and his harp.

expect to hear music the further we climb, but all is silent save for the clamor of a dozen men—brothers, I've decided—and their gassy mammoth pig. Nor do I see any majestic spires crowning the mountaintop, no godly glow or rosy, perfumed clouds.

Distrust begins to burgeon from the insatiable cavity of my anxiety, and as I follow the men upward I count them: fourteen heads the color of rudiwhit roots, raised like gooseflesh along the burnt sienna slope. Fourteen men and the Dagda's boar, and me trailing behind, my hair hastily knotted and my brow pebbled with sweat as I struggle up the steep incline, refusing to look away from my companions for fear one will slip out of sight.

I'm just beginning to regret my refusal of the boar's saddle when I notice smooth, unnatural planes of stone curving into the rockface above: a spiral staircase, wide enough to accommodate the boar's massive breadth. I watch as the strangely graceful beast traipses up the steps, her tail lashing like a whip as she disappears, up and away.

"Never seen a pig climb stairs before either, have ye?"

quips one of the men.

I cast him a look, but my words tunnel into a gasp when I notice, beyond his broad frame, the unending sky that drops off at the edge of the steps—stone beneath my feet, then a yawning nothingness.

I slap my hand against the rockface, pressing my side to it as if it will imbue my legs with stability or open up to hold me steady, but all it does is chill my fingertips. My unease feathers the air with condensation, and I try to slow my breathing, one stuttering inhale at a time until the paranoia eases its icy grip on my heels.

"Not far to go." The man still standing in front of me turns away, stamping hard on the steps as he goes.

I hurry to ascend in his wake, nails dug into the dough of my palm, staying near enough that he would have a chance to catch me were I to fall into the void. "Tread heavier, aye? The lot of you are shaking the mountain."

He looks over his shoulder to cock a thorny eyebrow at me, and to avoid looking beyond him again I focus on the blue of his eyes, finding within them an unexpected boyish fondness.

"I'm only showin' ye it's safe," he says. He stamps harder, both feet smacking the stone, wild curls bouncing turmoil against the cloudless scowl of night. "Rock can't be arsed t'move. Gobby could do a rain dance with the Lughs in steel armor atop 'er and the stubborn thing'll keep slumberin'."

I wince at his heavy-footedness but press the soles of my

124

feet more firmly upon the next step, reassured by its unwillingness to move. "Gobby—the she-boar?"

He nods. Faded ink teeth flash on the back of his neck. "And the Lughs...?"

"Three'a the knobs up ahead."

I focus on my knees bending, lifting, lowering, and on my ragged fingernail shearing away a callous to pierce the soft skin beneath. "And you?"

"Finín. Fin. Neenie. Eenie-meenie." He barks out a bitter-edged laugh. "Doesn't much matter when it's just Da and me brothers, the catatonic dullards. And Gobby, but she ha'n't talked since a warrior bull left 'er high and dry. Bless 'im, I was sick o' that crone singin' her woes. I reckon ye don't know how many woes a sow can have, do ye, girlie?"

"Can't say I do," I say, sparing my breath to keep my legs steady. One slip and my body would knife through the swollen mountain gloom and plunge to the earth a world below. I wonder what trees my blood would feed.

I wonder if Dìomath would mourn me.

As if sensing the straying of my thoughts, Finín pivots on one foot, swinging his other leg out over the edge of the stairs, making my toes curl.

"What is it you've come to beg o' the Dagda?" he asks.

"How do you know I've come to beg?"

With a shrug, he balances again on the edge of a step. "Move your feet—not far to go. It helps if ye loosen your buttocks. But no one comes for Da's mere company, not since 'e caught melancholy. It's a shame. We've more spirits than ever, more'n we know what to do with, really."

So at least that much is true, I think. Nathaire would be smug, with all his yap about the Dagda's guzzling craw.

"What do people come for, then?" I ask, feigning nonchalance, itching to pinch my fingertips but unwilling to take my hand from the immovable stone.

"To beg," Finín replies with a snort. "I dunnah—they think gods can do everythin', give 'em whatever they desire. Virgins askin' for babies, widows askin' for their husbands back." His head notches to the side, eyes slating askance toward me. "But I don't get the feelin' you have much want of either o' those things, eh?"

I run my tongue along my teeth and avert my gaze. "None at all. I find other needs more pressing."

"What sort o' needs?"

"Depends," I say wryly, "on what the Dagda *can* give. It doesn't sound like he can give much."

There's a long pause before Finín says anything, and when he speaks he sounds far away, his voice cramped with uncertainty.

"He's not the god 'e once was. Strangely enough, he's a better man for it."

*I*t must be nearing sunswake by the time a humble structure comes into view at the top of what was beginning to feel like an endless spiral of stairs. It takes my mind a moment to register the evenly stacked umber stones— squat pillars, snug against the mountain and leading into a small garden.

Most of the men having arrived long before me, I spy Éamon already bound against the sheer face of rock, and he chuffs at me as I stagger under a crumbling stone arch, grateful for the short wall now separating mountain from sky.

As I step over withered herbs and ungroomed roots, I notice among the poorly-kept yard a bush of hope roses, singularly thriving. Jarred, I reach out to touch its leaves, just to see if it's real, but am yanked away as I near.

Finín releases me quickly but shakes his head, solemn warning in his stare. "That's Da's."

I gesture to the rest of the garden. "Why is nothing else cared for?"

"Nothin' else is needed," he says. "And we haven't

much knack for carin' besides."

I frown as he walks ahead, casting another look at the bursting blooms of the hope roses—the vivacity of its life so strange in the blackened, broken yard—before following him through another set of taller columns, these leading into a firelit hall. One side is lined by pillars, moonswake slotted between, and the other is smooth mountainside flanking a wide opening.

The hall is otherwise empty save for a statue; a man and woman entangled in an embrace.

"Da and his mortal lover," Finín supplies, lingering near the opening into which his brothers disappeared. "She was of the flatlands. Died after Da defeated Cernunnos. All 'e talks about, and hasn't taken a mistress since."

I peer up at the woman's face, my gaze drawn to the squareness of her jaw, the wide stretch between her eyes, the crookedness of her mouth. Wild, unbraided hair. Broad shoulders, trunk-thick legs. Nothing delicate, nothing soft.

And the Dagda, cradling her like she's the loveliest thing in his garden.

I swallow hard to dislodge the lump in my throat—the itchy tightness I feel marrow-deep. I turn from the statue, too aware of my fingers fluttering along the features of my own face—jaw, forehead, mouth—but unable to stop myself, needing to feel the sharpness of it, to feel what Dìomath sees. The beauty I don't understand.

Finín clears his throat. "Alright, girlie?"

"Fine," I say with a nod. I suppress a wince at the

nickname but am unable to bring myself to correct him. "Lead on."

And so we pass into the rock maw of the so-called Palace of the Bees, which seems to me little more than a large cavern stuffed full of dark wood tables, all of them overflowing with food—more food than I've seen in my entire life, well enough all in one place. Heaps of steaming meat, shining with grease and honey. Fatty squid tentacles, golden-brown and speared on skewers. Swollen loaves of bread, bowls of mutton and juniper stew, potatoes bursting with leek, garlic, aubergine, and onion.

The assault of spices on my sense of smell intoxicates me, and I stand at the front of it all, gaping, possibly drooling, entirely uncaring. Even without having taken a bite, I feel as if I could fall into a stupor and sleep contentedly for days.

Finín chuckles and points across the cavern, where a bronze vat impressed with intricate patterns rests atop the highest table. "Da's cauldron never empties. Good thing, too, for a man who bears only sons, aye?"

A magical harp *and* a magical cauldron, yet their wielder uses neither for good. Were the puddings spread out before me not so tantalizing, I would be nauseated with anger at the thought.

I unabashedly steal up a bowl of I-don't-care-what and plunge a spoonful into my mouth, nearly coming undone as something sheerly ambrosial touches my tongue. Moaning with pleasure, I finish the bowl in moments and snatch up another.

"Where is he?" I ask Finín, finally having collected my thoughts and counting still only fourteen heads and two boars—one alive, one roasting—in the room.

Finín lifts his nose from a slab of meat, his beard dripping mead. "Preparin' his story, I reckon."

"His story?"

"The story of his greatest victory and his greatest defeat," he says simply. "They're the same, if ye hadn't guessed."

I scuff the back of my hand across my lips, wiping away the heavy oil left from my feasting. "What, he tells it every night?"

"Nae, girlie, only when 'e has guests. He knew ye were comin', that's why we came to get ye."

Not girlie, I think with a bristle, though his warm familiarity again stops me from giving my name—*Rhoswen* from his lips would sound too guttural, too sharp; nothing like the way Dìomath's tongue sweetens it.

"Let me guess: he has a magical watchtower, too."

Finín raises an eyebrow but makes no remark, or perhaps he does and I don't hear. Movement behind him distracts me—descending a crude flight of steps notched into the back of the cavern, a fifteenth head, enwreathed by a mass of the same tulsi-wine hair as the others. The same sky-jewel eyes, the same pink-sand skin. He is less naked than the other men, but what clothes he does wear are tattered and soiled.

"Da," utters one of the brothers, and it confirms the serpentine threshing in my belly.

I've found the Dagda.

$\mathcal{I}$ was but a child when I became Bearslayer. Though it should have been a suffocating weight upon me, it felt as if a burden had lifted. I had always been troubled by purposelessness, by an unyielding search for something beyond what I knew, something *other*, and becoming Hazelfeur's protector bestowed as much upon me—it gave me value.

But that fulfillment only lasted a single season, and when Artio's bears retreated to her lair at summer solstice each year, I would again find myself lost, wandering, starving on a plateau of dormancy. I was comfortable in my solitude but unnerved at the nexus of a busy village, one intent—obsessed, even—with animal-rearing and child-raising.

I found solace during these off-seasons in tending bearsbane bushes.

It was Onora who brought a palmful of the needled cuttings to me, harvested from the scrublands outside Hazelfeur, and she explained how the scent would ward off bears. For several days I contemplated the sprigs, watching the needles gradually spread apart, expanding as if to bare their souls to me.

It took little time for me to bare my soul in return.

recognize in the deep lines of the Dagda's face that same *wanting* I experienced, the glassiness of his gaze—beyond indicating his intemperance—revealing his struggle to fight through the iron cobwebs strung between his earlobes.

A god, in quiet despair.

I think of the rosebush in the courtyard; its startling brilliance; how it must be more obligation than need that drives him to maintain it. He is still wanting for something, and I can tell it is not flower-tending that will erase the sadness from his very essence.

A god, wanting for what?

While I contemplated the Dagda's apparent melancholy, he crossed the cavern, snatching a jug from one of the tables in a motion swift as breath, and now he stands before me, heavy-lidded and reeking of beer-stink and not at all what I imagined.

"What's this?" he asks, his voice like stripped timber left in the rain. His hand flaps vaguely toward my pelts. "Bearskin. Weren't ye in the company of a bear?" He sniffs in consideration. "I find this very perplexin'."

The snake in my belly has progressed up my throat, and I choke on my words. "Not a bear...there's a reason—I mean, a *reason*, being the reason I am...here..."

The Dagda doesn't seem to notice my incomprehensible mumbling. I clamp my mouth shut as he reaches down to my face—no, my hair. His fingers are short but thick, and gentle as a first snowfall as he twines a lock of my hair around his thumb.

"No' a girl atall," he murmurs, so quietly I'm certain I misheard him.

I realize after a moment that he's looking at me, hard, like I'm a drop of ale in a bottle he thought was empty, but I find it hard to meet his amorphous, watery gaze.

I pull away, pinching my fingertips.

Onetwothree.

The Dagda stands before me, and I've no idea what to do.

Onetwothree.

Has Hazelfeur fallen to the bears yet?

Onetwothreeonetwothreeonetwothree—

"I've come to ask for help," I say at last, touching the cord around my neck—the claw, the hair of the dead boy. "The bear goddess rains terror on my people."

The Dagda grunts, his eyes struggling to find purchase on my slippery gaze. It dawns on me I've been rude, forward, but I don't know any other way. Nor do I care for the mawk-ish smell of his ale-soaked beard.

"I am curious of yer story. Aye, more'n you may know." He blinks, and it is a blink that lasts a lifetime. He then takes a drink, and his thirst seems endless. "But first I tell *my* story. Fair?"

"I've heard your story," I tell him, sharpness lining my tongue. "Many of them, and none very interesting."

From around the cavern I hear the Dagda's sons gasp, more scandalized than Onora last springtide when I forewent her brightness, and the Dagda actually looks hurt. The creases around his mouth deepen, and the black shadows beneath his eyes darken until he looks sunken-in and haggard.

"Songs, I mean," I hurry to amend, worried he may cast me out. "I've heard songs of your conquests. Your story is...more compelling, I'm sure."

"Songs? *Bah.*" The Dagda hawks up a gob of saliva and spits it at his feet. "Godsdamned music. I'd just as 'appily eat a rock than hear a note o' music again."

"Is strumming a harp truly so hard?"

His brows twitch, steepling above a crooked nose. "What're you on about? Nay, I just hate the noise. Loud. And for what, eh? Glamoured words, false emotions. Stuff o' deceit."

I frown, wanting to press him about Ràithne, but I wonder already if I've aroused his suspicions. If I'm to steal away his celestial harp, I must first make good company.

And to make good company with this maudlin god and his unclothed sons, I need my soothing thing.

Once the Dagda and the brothers have feasted, the boar settles on a mound of furs in the crook of the cavern. With a freshly-steeped bowl of heady goldroot tea, I follow the men as they withdraw from the cavern and congregate in the pillared hall clinging to the mountain's side. The brothers sit cross-legged along the walls, broad shoulders pressed together, a copper-topped palisade. Where they had looked like men before, they now look like boys, faces softened by the rapture with which they regard their father.

The Dagda.

A conniving bastard, said Dìomath.

No mercy nor love in his heart.

Seduces women, tricks them, rapes them.

Fools mortals into thoughts that are not their own.

Slipping to the ground beside Finín, I reach to pluck at my eyebrow, but find little hair left to pluck and instead scratch at the mossiness coating my teeth. The bowl in my lap warms my thighs, and I long to drink of it; to thaw the rime, the frosty blight upon my mind.

But I would be a fool to disregard my enchantress's warning.

For her sake I must remain clearheaded—I only struggle to discern whether my relentless worries are more muddling than the goldroot.

While my breath remains steady, I decide, I will not partake of the tea, and so I thread my fingers into a tight knot and look—with more skepticism than his sons—upon the Dagda.

He stands next to the statue, though the chiseled features and sharp glare of his sculpted counterpart bear little likeness to him now, with clouded eyes and a face like melting wax.

And then I see the air fill his lungs, and the Dagda tells his tale.

She wasn't cruel as he knew her.

He thought it providence, that day he came down from his palace, homesick though he had a mountain to call home. When he left, none of his sons had begged him to stay.

He had gone to the sea first, felt the salt on his cheeks and the sand between his toes. But he felt no kinship, no sense of belonging under the seaspray. Wondering if perhaps he should build a boat and cut across the oceans to the lands beyond, tired of the responsibility this land demanded of him, he asked a coiled shell if great love awaited him on this rock.

Not here, replied the conch, there—and squinting along its length he saw where the shell pointed.

The forest.

He made haste for the trees, their greenery bright as a balefire, the lands to the west nothing more than a subdued blur, surely nothing of interest. And coming upon the forest, giddy in anticipation of what he might find, he saw her.

The deceitress, as he would come to call her.

But she was no deceitress then, no. She was beautiful, radiant. When he looked upon her he felt warm, and wondered what it would feel like to touch her. What it would be to love her.

He's unsure now, which of them seduced the other—he supposes it doesn't matter, only that together they were a rapture, a beginning and an end.

And then she unraveled before him.

She had been alone for an eternity, exiled by her father, cast to the neglect of those hallowed woods.

She had only been healing, she said of her crimes; resurrecting her dead children. Her father's horn had allowed it, granted new life, and how could life be wrong?

But her father had banished her, reviled by the disruption she caused to the world he kept so carefully balanced, and so she was to remain in these woods for all the eternities to come, made to watch her children grow old and die, grow old and die, grow old and die.

After hearing her woes, he was filled with rage. He knew of her father, had harbored no ill will toward him, but soon envisioned himself tearing the man limb from limb—if not for keeping such *a lovely maiden trapped in the confines of a loveless, sunless wood, then for carrying himself like the godliest of them all, when it was he in fact who bore the weight of divinity's power.*

He vowed to avenge her, free her, and obtain the father's horn so she could be with her children once more.

She told him her heart was his, and he took it, not knowing the evils contained within.

For a moment the Dagda ceases his tale, and in that pause I feel weightless, dizzied by his somber narration, his history, perhaps legend but not myth, all of it a spellbinding curse.

He found the father in a small village, a piece of the blur he had raced past in his haste for great love. The father's power was evident in the bursting buds of plants once dead, traces of their first life streaked black at the roots. Flowers shivering with growth, petals humming as they stretched too wide in their rebirth. Trees depositing fat nuts into sprites' baskets at a pace they could not hope to keep up with.

A nature god's magick—the same magick for which the daughter had been banished.

He did not contain his rage.

He waged war.

The father was old, his deityhood forgotten but to this village and its flora, and even they seemed to have tired of him. Certainly, they had tired of his sprites, those ugly, greedy, thieving creatures over which the father exerted little control. Always letting nature do as it pleased.

And so the village took his side. They were not versed in battle, but they did what they could, offering him their hearths, their homes, their hands where he could use them. The deceitress, too, sent him aid: her living children, not cursed as she was to remain in the woods. What the villagers lacked in bloodlust, the children made up for in their unbridled aggression.

But with the tricky sprites on the father's side, the battle was far from a simple feat. The old god strangled the village with his horn's magick: long-forgotten roots burst forth from the ground, trapping villagers in their homes or driving them into the yellowed teeth of hungry sprites. Tangles of vines once hacked away from the crops rose again, descending to sink mighty thorns into the children's eyes.

There was ruin wrought by new life; horror in the father's so-called balance.

The war lasted months, young god against old god.

Long enough for him to find another great love—this one a mortal woman, a wild beauty formed under the sun and the stars.

Here the Dagda regards the statued woman, his hand fitting under her chin so perfectly it's as if the stone was molded to his very touch. Were his own statue not frozen in the woman's embrace, I feel he would sweep the maiden into his arms and she would live once more.

It is all part of the tale—of *then*, not now.

He came to treasure the mortal woman as one would treasure gold, but she was a currency he would never trade for better, for to him she was the pinnacle—the salt, the sea, the sun. She was cataclysmic, an ecstasy of totality, a violently ruinous tempest.

The deceitress remained in his heart, as it was she for whom he bled, but when he lay with the mortal woman, she eclipsed all else.

And soon, deep within her, a murmur.

By spring's end, he had worn the deceitress's father to his brown, brittle bones; had torn the crown of antlers from the old god's head and the life-giving horn from his withered lips. The father's defeat was swift, a clean blow that rang with the finality of a closing tomb.

The sprites fought on for a time, vengeful in their desire to avenge the god to which they had pledged allegiance, but soon surrendered, retreated, seethed. They left—but they would be back.

When the mortal woman begged him to rest, he indulged her. They slept, caressed, loved. She unbraided his hair and pressed kisses to his scars. He whispered to the murmur in her belly and sang of his love.

Deciding he had kept the deceitress waiting long enough, still yearning to free her of her forested prison and deliver her the means to be with her children once more, he made to leave.

But the mortal woman—having seen the father wield the magickal horn and perceived its dark power—implored that he hide the horn so no one could abuse the cycle of life. She led him around the village, showed him the deceitress's fallen children.

She would have them suffer through life, having already known death? *she asked of him, and looking upon the slain he understood.*

To be mortal was to be a subject of death. To come back from that was unfathomable.

And so he took the old god's horn and buried it far, far, far beneath the battlefield the village had become. Then over the earth he cast an enchantment such that the horn could not be raised but by the strum of his harp by his daughter's hand. By this he was ensuring the land would never be broken, for he bore only sons.

The father's horn would remain in the earth.

What he didn't notice as he broke his deceitress's faith were the eyes watching him; the old god's allies—the sprites—hadn't gone far, and devoted as they were to the old god's bloodline, they took the news of his enchantment to the god's daughter.

To the deceitress they divulged the details of her father's death and her lover's betrayal.

So, too, did they reveal what the mortal woman carried in her womb.

The Dagda stops for a third time to nurse his drink. As his head tilts back, the dark tracks beneath his eyes are illuminated, and I know they were carved by misery. They once carried rivers.

She was cruel in the end.

So very, very cruel.

The spell is broken with the crack of the Dagda's voice. He seems suddenly small and fragile, the chasms hewn into his face emphasized by the firelight, wrinkles wrought not by age but by a feral, deathless pain.

This god is still but a gentle man.

She became the deceitress then, by what she ordered of her father's sprites.

They returned to the village quietly, slipping in while the dead were lifted onto the Sun Stone; while death still prowled the injured and grief numbed the senses of the living.

The sprites stole in under the muted blanket of sorrow, intending to add to its threads those of the young god who would stay to see the village rebuilt.

They murdered his great love.

He woke to her coldness beside him, her sun-browned skin marbled and bloodless.

The mortal woman was not beautiful in death. No, she had been mutilated horribly, and he wished he could drown in the blood weeping from her carved belly, from her cruelly emptied womb. No, there was nothing beautiful in this death. There was nothing at all.

With little regard for any peril the little village found itself in under the reign of the sprites, nor for the desolation he had promised to mend—truly, with little regard for anything but his own agony—he took his leave of the mortal lands.

It was true, he had found what he had come for, but it had been far too precious, that transient tragedy of human life, so easily crumbling to meaninglessness even while his love persisted.

Even while his love would persist for eternity.

he Dagda's sons remain silent as ever when he finishes his tale, and the hall is so quiet that I wonder if they still hold their breath as I do. Even the wind from the gorge beyond the pillars has hushed, the ratty mountain-brush untouched and soundless for a time, mindful of the Dagda's long-past yet ever-present loss.

My blood hums, my fingernails cutting petals into my kneecaps.

I knew his story—or at least knew parts of it, while other parts rang with eerie familiarity.

A forest maiden, a village, its sprites.

Questions sprout like mushrooms in my mind, but it feels wrong to press them upon the Dagda, who still stands with his hand affixed to the statue, his face drawn in a way that makes it clear he has not yet returned from his tale.

But, no longer transfixed by his voice, my anxieties rear their ugly heads. Pressure builds within me, and I feel trapped among the brothers, feel their stench as if it sits upon my chest.

I wriggle around, trying to find an unimpeded pocket of

air, worried my aching legs will fall dead if I don't move them and yearning for the woody smell of home and a beautiful face—

In my jostling, though I try to be inconspicuous, I knock the bowl of goldroot tea to the ground. In a golden spray, it collides horrendously with the statue's plinth, spattering the depiction of the Dagda, darkness seeping into the unpolished stone.

The brothers remain silent, perhaps rendered speechless by my clumsiness, and the quiet only serves to make everything worse. Why don't they speak? Why don't they scold me? Why won't they break this godsforsaken silence?

I stand awkwardly; I don't want to, but I'm overcome with a restless unease evoked by the Dagda's story. I should have drunk the tea while it remained unspilt.

The Dagda looks at the bowl, which rolls on the ground to mock me, and then he laughs and laughs and laughs, huge rounded peals of thunder that aren't without humor yet sound formidable, predatory. It reminds me of a feral badger stuck in a well.

"Da hates his statue," Finín says—*finally*—over the god's howling. He clambers to his feet. "He's thrown worse at it. Has had some right nasty fits, tell ye the truth. Once 'e bludgeoned it with his harp, tryin' to break them both, but his effects are hardy. Neither got so much as a scratch. Even the might o' Gobby in heat wasn't enough—"

"He tried to break Ràithne?" I interrupt, shocked. "But what of the seasons? What would happen without her song?"

Finín joins his father in laughter but ceases his blessedly quick. "What on earth are ye on about?"

"The—your father's harp. Ràithne. Season's harbinger. He plays her, and the seasons obey, do they not? We...dance for him." I glance at the Dagda, thankful to see his laughter slowing. "We dance for the Dagda."

Finín only stares, then claps me on the shoulder and turns, hooting, "Da! Did ye know the mortals *dance* for ye?"

The Dagda laughs so hard his face grows as red as his hair.

I t is nearly sunswake by the time the Dagda has sobered, and back inside the cavern I approach him hesitantly, praying the mere sight of me doesn't send him into another fit.

"Hazelfeur," I say upon nearing his table, still unsure how to address this god-man-storyteller, and the Dagda looks up drowsily. "The village in your tale. Was it Hazelfeur?"

He sighs heavily. "Aye, it was. I imagine there's not much left of it."

"They made a pact with the púca—we make sacrifices to them, even still, and in return they leave us be. I didn't know why they would do such a thing, but now, without a god to tell off the beasts...I suppose I do."

"That's dangerous business," the Dagda grunts, his concern a mere pulse in his cheek, gone in an instant. He takes a drink, but most of the ale streams into his beard and seeps into crusted bits of bread that would make Nathaire reel in disgust.

I grind my molars together and the sound is crisp,

certain. "And the forest...deceitress. What was her name?"

His eyes harden with black wrath. "The same *goddess*—" he spits the word like venom, "who gives you trouble, flatlander. We needn't speak her name. Deceitress will do."

"Artio," I say, my voice bolder than I feel. "She may be a deceitress, but by refusing to say her name, you fail to give it the ill repute it deserves. Artio was the one who had your lover killed—your child killed—and now she wages war on my people. The children she raised with her father's horn still terrorize us, along with their living brothers."

The Dagda leans back, a cool flicker of intrigue breaking apart the steel in his gaze. He considers me. "It was one o' her bears in your company. One o' her children."

"Aye, but her daughter sent him with me for safety—"

"Her daughter?" he asks, scowling with a heavy brow. "What, a human daughter?"

I clamp my mouth shut, still wishing for my enchantress to remain a secret—*my* secret. Shaking my head, I say, "It's Hazelfeur she's waging war on. Artio is still seeking revenge for *your* affairs."

The Dagda shoves the table forcefully, spilling drinks and sending bowls and baskets spilling to the floor. He stands, fire in his eyes, his jaw, his demeanor.

My cheeks flush, and I begin to babble an apology, not having meant to inspire his temper with accusations, but then I stop myself.

"Do you think I'm wrong?" I ask, still sounding too bold for the fervid quaking of my innards. Were it not for the

168

rose brooch at my throat, I fear I would shake free of my skin. *What a sight my gore would make, spilled before a drunken god.*

The Dagda sways, knocks away a still-standing jug, then pitches forward to brace his hands on the table.

Bent over and brooding without dignity, I see his hair at the root is more silver than red, his forehead crushed by wrinkles, and I wonder if I've misjudged what it means to be divine.

"There are many evils in this world, aren't there? I never thought I'd be among them," he murmurs, his fingers curled bone-white against the wood's grain like two halves of a ribcage. "I never wanted ta hurt them—but humans are fallible creatures. Unfortunate slaves to mortality, full o' dreams and tragedies. I felt what it was to be mortal. I felt the weight o' their insignificance, and it shouldn't'a hurt me as it did. Deities aren't *meant* to feel that way." He moans. "I know wi' absolute certainty I'll not find joy again. Tell me, what would ye do if ye felt as I do?"

I swallow, but it does nothing to bring words forth, and I stand there dumbly, torn between pity and loathing.

"You came to beg my help," the Dagda says, "but I cannot help them, whether I brought such horror upon them or not. But the deceitress? She will stop at nothin' for her freedom and for her birthright."

"I've gathered as much," I say quietly. I press closer to the table, stooping low, trying to catch his gaze. "You've known grief, but haven't you also known love? I've known love—perhaps not great but it doesn't matter the size. These things we *mortals* feel are painful. But they are all we know, and I will not stop fighting for them."

The words flowed out with the rush of a dying secret, ragged and raw, but they were enough to make the Dagda look up. Gone is the anguish from his face, replaced by a frown not of revelation but rather confusion.

"You think you're mortal, child?"

As night becomes day I am no closer to understanding what the Dagda claims is truth.

That I am neither human nor god, but a creation of both.

It's all he says, that he knows I am not mere mortal, but immediately I grapple to find a foundation for his words; for my being more than I was moments ago.

It's too much, this being something else, and I despise the Dagda for burdening me with the knowledge.

Perhaps it's not true. How could it be?

Mine is not a story of poignance.

"Told ye he's not much one for givin' anymore."

I look up to see Finín walk across the courtyard, where I had come in my shock to plunge my fingers into the ashy soil and seek out diseased roots; to feel the earth sway all around me, its great heaving breaths making my own unsteadiness sufferable.

"He's a selfish, spudheaded sot," I scoff. "But it's not him I came for."

Finín chews on his lip. "So you're leavin', then?"

I gently dig around the base of a dead plant and shake the tangle of roots free of dirt clods. "I can't stay any longer. I must return to protect my people—and besides, surrounded by the fools here, I fear I'll become one myself."

"We're not *all* fools," he says, shifting uncomfortably. "Da isn't foolish. The melancholy is a disease, girlie, and he's been taken with it worse than that feverfew you've got. And I think ye know somethin' of diseases o' the mind."

Without meaning to, I squeeze the feverfew, and my fingers break through brittle branches like age-old wraith bones. I shoot Finín a glare. "And yet, *I* am here, doing what

173

I can for those in peril, and without a vice to get me through it."

"What of that tea ye made?"

I return my attention to the plant, taking Thornfury's blade to the root rot. "I don't rely on the tea to get me through the day as your father does with his mead. Besides, I spilled the damn stuff."

"Da's a considerable storyteller, int he?" Finín asks, but when he rubs the back of his neck, I get the sense he's hedging at something more than the Dagda's tale.

"Fin," I start, feeling it finally safe to broach the subject of that for which I came to this mountain, "your Da—his harp. Does he not play her?"

He shakes his head.

"Not ever?"

"Not since 'e returned from the flatlands. Said if he couldn't spin songs for his mortal lover, 'e couldn't spin songs at all. Trust me, it's for the better—he's an awful harpist. His fingers might as well be rolls o' pigmeat. The instrument must be made for women, though we wouldn't know. Gobby's certainly never taken to it." He chuckles.

I trap my tongue between my teeth, crawling across the garden with the withered feverfew to replant it out of shadow. "But does she...does the harp have magic?"

"Oh, o' course," he says, sitting on the short wall as he watches me scrape away soil, a glimmer of far-off sea gilding the horizon beyond him. "Your folk tales aren't unfounded, but Da strummin' Ràithne doesn't bring the seasons'

174

change. Well, it *can*, but the seasons'll change in their natural order regardless. Damn shame, innit, that we can't forgo winter?"

"Couldn't we, though? Could your Da not make it so?"

Finín considers, idly scrubbing a toe through the dirt. "I suppose. But why would 'e want to do such a thing?"

"If he were to turn from autumn to spring, eluding winter entirely," I muse, "crops would never suffer, food wouldn't become scarce."

He blinks, uncomprehending.

"Unlike you and your kin, us mortal—" I wince, trying not to think of the Dagda's claims of my lineage, "—*flatlanders* have no ever-flowing puddings or meat pies. We struggle to survive, and not only winter but spring as well. Spring is our waking nightmare."

Finín's foot stills, interrupting the spiral his toe had been tracing in thought. He slides off the wall to kneel opposite me, his forehead furrowed. "Ye really didn't come for Da, did ye? Ye came for Ràithne."

I avert my gaze, tucking the feverfew's newly trimmed roots into the hollow I dug. "Does it surprise you? That I thought a harp would be better aid than your father."

"It's refreshin', tell ye the truth," he admits. He helps pat loose soil. "I love my Da dearly, but he's not as worthy o' faith as 'e once was. It's taken me a long time to see it—blind are boys to their born heroes, aye? His feats have grown dusty, and now mortals come and go wi' their prayers unanswered." His sigh is hauntingly empty. "What's the difference between gods and heroes, do ye think?"

"Heroes live for something bigger than themselves. Gods...gods only yearn to be bigger." I shake my head, tiring of such talk, unwilling to any further taint Finín's admiration of his father, and even less willing to give further thought to a deity so undeserving.

"But yes," I say, standing to give the feverfew space to breathe, "I came for Ràithne. I can't ask you not to tell your Da, for you owe me nothing. I can only hope you'll grant me a little time before you do."

Finín tucks a finger into his beard to scratch his chin, eyes flickering. "You mean ta steal his harp?"

"It hardly sounds like he'll miss her."

"Just because 'e can't bear to play her doesn't mean she int precious to 'im. As ye well know, Ràithne is highly revered, and for good reason. The druids carved 'er from the first oak this earth sprouted. Her adornments were gifts from the wizards whom Da led ta victory against the sea raiders—"

"Leaving her sat upon a shelf is doing all her glory justice, aye?" I ask. I feel the fire in me giving way to ice, hear it in the waver of my voice. "She could be of veritable help to my people. And your father was not in the least swayed by pleas for aid."

Finín shakes his head. "It wouldn't matter, girlie—stolen or nae, you'd not be able to play her. She only obeys Da's blood."

For a moment I wither, my hopes succumbing to the

oppressive crush of desperation, but then the cresting sun haloes Finín's head, crowning him with a familiar air of divinity.

"She would heed your pigmeat fingers, then. And you..." I realize I have nothing to offer him and swallow hard before continuing. "Would you care to depart from your dullard brothers for a time?"

inín's answer is noncommittal, but his face is bright as he leads me without ado across the cavern, babbling about his farthest forays down the mountain around mouthfuls of cheese.

"The Lughs wouldn't come wi' me, but I went anyway. I thought it was a wee leprechaun, see, and I was in need of a wish since Naoise had fooled me out o' my best pair'a britches. There've been leprechauns before, it int unheard of, we even found a nest of 'em once pilferin' from Da's best spirits.

"So I followed the leprechaun, and I asked for a wish, and 'e said he would grant me three if I retrieved somethin' for him from a pool a ways down the mountain. O' course I obliged—he was very charmin' and had the jolliest little face. I went to the pool, and I took off my remainin' clothin' and dove in. In winter, mind ye. I reckon I can't sire sons now for the chill o' it.

"I splashed about in that pool for half the night, but found nothin', so I finally gave up, only ta find my clothes were gone. *All* of 'em. Had ta come all the way back arse naked and blue. The leprechaun was nowhere ta be found—still dunnae if it was a leprechaun at all. Roguish beastie, whatever it was.

"The followin' moons, my brothers encountered similar creatures offerin' similar bargains, and o' course they obliged, if not for the wishes then ta rub their genius in my face. But one by one they, too, came back robbed o' their clothes."

I snort at the absurdity of the story, and the gravity in Finín's voice as he tells it, but can hardly fault them for falling prey to faerie trickery.

"So that's why you're so sparsely dressed?" I ask, unable to keep the humor from my voice.

He nods, still somber but for the glint in his blue eyes. "Wouldn't stop me from pursuin' wishes again, though. I have less clothes ta lose these days." With a smirk, he stops at the far end of the cavern, where the high table bows under the weight of the Dagda's ever-full eldritch cauldron.

Behind the table, I notice an alcove, the darkness within winking with treasure. I cast Finín a questioning look, and he nods but makes no move to enter. He shifts his weight, sneaking furtive glances around the cavern like an overgrown, bearded child caught throwing pebbles at the púca's temple.

"I think I'll...wait outside," he mutters.

"Would you free Éamon for me?" I ask. "He's mild-mannered."

He thinks for a moment, plucking at his beard, then dips

his chin to his bare chest and turns to hurry back across the cavern, weaving around the lumpy forms of his still-sleeping brothers. Before disappearing into the outer hall, he takes a step toward the tiny staircase—above which I imagine the Dagda's quarters bedecked in plump cushions and discarded goblets—then shakes his head and ducks outside.

I suck in a breath, count thirteen pairs of closed eyelids to ensure that none of the brothers are feigning sleep, and slip into the dimly lit alcove.

I expect to see Ràithne immediately, bejeweled and displayed grandly on a pedestal befitting of legend, but the area is cluttered with artifacts. Hunching to see where I step, I pick through stacks of tomes, careless piles of pottery, chests carved with depictions of deities, bands of metal —perhaps crowns once but now warped beyond recognition—and a scattering of clubs and swords long-unused.

Finally, behind a cluster of stained baskets holding an assortment of yellowed vials, I spy the gentle arch of twisted wood; an austere instrument, its apex no higher than my shoulder, inlaid not with jewels but with smooth stones of muted color, its strings made not of stretched gold but of simple horsehair.

I reach out to touch her, rather uninspired by her appearance and uncertain that such a mundane thing could possibly wield power enough to save Hazelfeur.

As my fingers brush the wizened wood, I realize I've been unaffected in my nearness: no hysterics, no laughter, no sudden rips in the fabric of my sanity.

Doubtful that this is truly Ràithne, I search the cave again, more reckless this time, barbs of panic prickling behind my eyes. I think of calling for Finín, needing assurances that under his touch the harp will come to life, but then I hear movement, a clattering behind me.

I whirl in time to see a flash of auburn go around the corner, and I hear frenzied footsteps thump out across the main cavern—one of the brothers, alerting the Dagda of my thievery.

"Danu's *tits*," I hiss, pinching my fingertips, my cursed legs frozen in place. I snatch up the unassuming harp; it's heavier than I expected, and had I the time I would look for a means of strapping it to my back. But I don't have the time, so I heft maybe-Ràithne as best I can and force myself to move.

As I drag the harp out of the alcove and past the high table, I see the Dagda descending his steps unsteadily, glassy eyes on me. He doesn't look angry, only confused, that perpetual undercurrent of misery lingering beneath.

"Ye...ye're alright," he says haltingly, but I'm far enough that I can't tell if it's a question or an observation.

Before either of us has the chance to move or say anything further, there comes a furied roar from the cavern's entrance, the sound of a beast with a thirst for needless blood.

By the sound of it, Éamon is not as mild-mannered as I thought.

amon's roar jars me into action, and maybe-Ràithne drops to the ground with a thud as I replace her with Thornfury's chain, prepared to swing should the fleshbear charge me.

However, Éamon directs his attack not at me but at the brothers, most of whom have just roused from sleep and struggle in their grogginess to untangle their legs from furs and blankets.

The first of them doesn't even manage to get to his feet before Éamon strikes him down, and I know at once the brother will not rise.

An outcry of broken rage fills the cavern. The other brothers surge forward, unarmed and unarmored, vulnerable in the onset of such sudden agony. I see the Dagda reach out as if to stop them, and then he's falling down the steps and crumpling at their base.

I have little concern for the god, though, and instead rush to help his sons. By the time I've leapt across the tables and reached the fray, five more brothers have fallen.

"*Éamon!*" I scream, knowing it unlikely that the bear will

hear reason but fearing what Dìomath would feel were I to slay the kin she entrusted to my care. "Stop! *Leave!*"

Éamon pays me no mind and dips his long claws into another son of Dagda, and another, the blood of the brothers only seeming to amplify his thirst, driven to kill them as if to do so is in the construct of his bones.

And so I let Thornfury fly.

It's difficult to say what happens next, only that one moment Thornfury's scythe is slicing soundlessly through the stifling air, and the next he's trapped under Éamon's massive paw, chain snapping taut and yanking me off my feet.

Then I'm sprawled in a mess of stew and crockery, my chin planted in splattered pudding that only serves to sour my mouth with bile. As I lift my head, dazed, I find myself level with an unseeing pair of eyes and a too-still mass of curls.

I gasp and draw myself up, vomit on my tongue and crimson fringing my vision.

I tug at Thornfury's chain, but the scythe remains planted under the fleshbear's full weight even as Éamon swipes at the few remaining brothers—who still surge forward without fear, blind in their need for vengeance.

Without Thornfury, I am useless, once again that unbloodied maiden hovering, untethered, at the bounds of purpose.

Éamon lifts his paw, freeing my blade, but before I can drag it back into my grip, he snaps the chain up in his jaw.

Not without shame, I cower as he charges past me. Only with the realization that the Dagda's living blood dwindles do I uncurl myself and stagger to my feet, sprinting for the cavern's mouth. At the threshold of the outer hall, I glance over my shoulder, cursing my untamed hair from my eyes.

The Dagda is still where he fell at the base of the steps, and though he still lives I see in his expression as he looks upon his fallen sons that he wishes he didn't. His empty gaze roves over me, the depths of his soul bared in those two darkened voids like blackened seeds.

Seeds that will never bloom.

Éamon crashes into the high table where I abandoned Ràithne, and the giant boar squeals, finally startled from deep pig-sleep. The clangor pierces the sepulchral moment of calm, and I take my leave of the Dagda's ruined palace. Passing the statue where the Dagda told his tale only hours ago, I burst into the garden in search of Finín, hoping to drag him down the mountain before my enchantress's kin can sink his lancelike claws into Hazelfeur's last hope.

I see the feverfew first, its leaves—this morning withered and browned—already perked and fleecy. Then I see the bindings with which the brothers had restrained Éamon, shredded and strewn, and among them a body similarly savaged.

Facedown in the dirt and pale as tundra, it could have been any of the brothers but for the watery ink on his neck—a wolf with fourteen pointed teeth.

A horrible noise rips through and out of me, the sound

a fulmination of hopelessness; of a whole village perishing; of the crows that will pick our bones clean.

I cannot hear anything over the hot rush in my ears, cannot feel anything but the pain searing across my spine— the same ragged wounds scored upon Finín's back, only phantoms of the agony I am sure he felt.

With his death, so too comes Hazelfeur's.

Nathaire, Onora, her children, the elders—perhaps even the púca, though I find no comfort in the thought.

I have failed them all.

I don't hear Éamon come up behind me, hardly feel his teeth scrape like steel against my shoulder blades. I find myself suddenly facing the sky, something both hard and soft beneath me, but only think that I should've rolled Finín onto his back so he, too, could appreciate the petalled clouds, the blue-grey brindle, and its promise of freedom.

After a time, I find the strength to roll over and face what must be my death. I wonder if it will be that cliffside drop into the Palace of the Bees' fatal cradle. I wonder if that is what I would prefer, to die a coward's death, screaming into endless oblivion rather than that more righteous death, the one I always expected. A Bearslayer's death.

But the death I face is not what I expected—it is not death at all, but a harp.

My shoulder is pressed into the crook of her wood, my cheek pillowed by her strings. With a frown, I touch one of the stones embedded within the wood, and it is as smooth as the sea.

"Ràithne," I murmur. "How...?"

It is not she who answers, but Éamon, with a familiar ornery grunt.

I snap my hand to my hip, unnerved to find my belt unburdened, remembering I lost Thornfury to the same beast that I now realize carries me and the Dagda's harp.

"You bastard *beast*!" I scream, fisting my hands into the fur of his nape and wrenching with all the force I can muster. "You were to *help* me, not murder them all, you horrid worm-slime spawn of—"

Éamon bucks fiercely and I gasp, quickly aware of the chasmal stretch of grey to my right. Deciding that it is *not* a coward's death I want, I pull myself flush against the bear's back, hooking my arm around Ràithne for good measure.

I stay like that, a helpless passenger clinging to my unpredictable mount as it hurtles down the mountain, leaving behind the only soul that could serve as Hazelfeur's savior, hopeless as he may be.

Why Éamon stole the harp I cannot guess—perhaps Artio thinks herself capable of harnessing Ràithne's powers and Dìomath, unwitting of her mother's manipulations, sent the She-Bear's servant to retrieve it for her. Perhaps Artio yearns for an eternal spring, whereas I aimed to eliminate the season altogether.

As for why I ever contemplated giving such cunning bearspawn bum rubs, I am even less certain.

At Éamon's pace, it is scarcely past high sunswake before we've left the Palace of the Bees behind. I've long since decided against throwing myself from his back or attempting to snatch Thornfury from his teeth, deciding instead to see where he takes me. My last lingering hope is that he delivers me to Artio herself, that he deposits me at her feet and with poetic, rightful violence, I can crack Ràithne upon her skull and end it all.

Ropes of dread weave through my ribcage, drawing my chest tighter and tighter as we pass through the heathered moors, my eyes fixed on the horizon, waiting for the cluster of tapered straw roofs to rise above the scrubby brush.

Two nights have passed since I left my people to the mercy of Artio's children. I have little faith that they showed any restraint in my absence—if Artio knew the Bearslayer was gone, she would have sent the full force of her brood to set ruin to Hazelfeur. And though I trust Dìomath to have kept the knowledge of my departure from her mother, I harbor no misgivings that Artio has other means of knowing such things.

I worry for what I will find, or if there will be anything left to find at all.

For a moment I succumb to the morbid thought; I let myself wonder, were Hazelfeur to have fallen, what I would become. To be Bearslayer wouldn't mean anything without a people to protect from the bears. Even tending my bearsbane bushes would be for naught and hunting for food little more than a game.

I wonder, were Dìomath to allow me to love her, if that could be my purpose.

Perhaps it would be selfish, to love her. For that to be my sole responsibility. But it also intoxicates me, the idea of her as enchantress and me, enchantee.

I shake my head bitterly, plunging my teeth into my tongue. As exhilarating as it would be, an eternal consorting of Bearslayer and She-Bear's daughter is the stuff of dreams—in this reality, so long as Artio lives, it would be impossible.

For now, at least, I still have purpose, and that purpose draws ever near.

Thorn's
FURY

The late afternoon sun watches as Éamon tosses me from his back and I tumble to the ground without dignity, Ràithne landing heavily and with only a touch more respect beside me.

I sit up warily, watching the bear as he drops Thornfury. Strings of scarlet saliva stretch between his maw and the scythe, snapping only when Éamon licks his teeth and releases a wet huff.

Then he turns and takes off toward Bairnhart Forest.

Scrambling to my feet, I seize Thornfury, intending to pursue the murderous beast and remove his head. What stops me is the blood of the Dagda's sons, slick under my grip; a reminder that their deaths are on my hands.

Instead of giving chase, I consider Ràithne—though I have no means of using her, it feels wrong to leave her so ignobly discarded in a thatch of weeds. As unassuming as she seems, something about her calls to me. I long to hear her song.

I strap Thornfury to his proper place at my hip, then lean down to heft Ràithne across my shoulders. Her weight seems less noticeable, and assuming it must be the surge of adrenaline pushing me to return to my people, I make haste across the scrublands.

The smothering ether of time leeches away at my courage the farther I run. My scalp itches under the hot weight of my hair, which, drenched in sweat, whips at my face with enough force to leave welts. I must look like a madwoman, the squally state of my mane all too indicative of the state of my mind.

So, too, does my hair evoke the image of the Dagda's sons, curls splayed like blood spray, fireheart-blue eyes clouded in death.

Did any of them live?

My chest twists, wringing out a gasp as I think of the god's empty gaze, of the deepening lines in his face as I left him to face the ruin of all he had left.

There's a strange moment as the memory of Éamon, body unfurled like a spear, is at once imprinted on the backs of my eyelids and stretched out suddenly before me, a mass of fur rippling toward an ivory point—claws.

A colossal fleshbear flashes across the scrublands, crashing through the brush without regard for the new life blooming, crushing flowering dwarf shrubs underfoot and bowling through tufted gorse bushes.

I watch as the beast soars over the decrepit stone wall.

I watch as its feet land in a bed of golden roses.

I watch as more of its kind erupt from the woods.

I watch as bears swarm toward Hazelfeur.

$\mathcal{I}$, too, leave broken stems in my wake as I sprint in vain toward my village.

There's a strange silence, as if even the groan of the earth turning has ceased, but a hum at the base of my skull rumbles with the ghostly echo of screams shed not long ago.

My people's screams.

Ràithne slams uncomfortably against my shoulder as I run until finally I abandon her at the edge of the village, the derelict state of which I try not to despair at. I stumble through the fresh ruins of a roundhouse—Èilde Malvynn's, I dully comprehend as the jagged nib of a carved stag stabs into my heel—and, with a leap, swing Thornfury into the first hunk of bear I fall upon.

It dawns on me as I hack into the wraithbear's rotting flesh that I'm not wearing any bearsbane. What few blood-crusted sprigs remain woven through Thornfury's chain rattle to the ground when it snaps taut.

Fleetingly distracted as I watch the needles fall, I give the wraithbear all it needs. In a flurry of cold, charnel air it descends, brittle bones whispering, savage splinters of bone knocking into my ribs.

But the blow—and the pain that accompanies it—gives *me* all I need.

I feel neither noble nor godly, only angry.

With the rage flowing through my veins, I am neither deity nor demideity.

With my anger, I am viciously, horribly human.

A scream rips through me, but it's not one of fear. It is a climatic sound of the mouth and lungs, of the eyes and soul; a sound that requires no answer, no control, no repression. For a moment it's a scream, then a laugh, then a cry—it doesn't matter. It is release.

Thornfury slices through festering black fur, through sooty, scabrous gristle, through spongy bones that crumble to ash, and the wraithbear falls with a terrible shriek. Guided by the snap of my wrist, Thornfury's blade then finds the meat of a fleshbear and cuts through skin and muscle like water.

As a third bear falls under my silver scythe, I catch sight of the Sun Stone through a cluster of still-standing huts. The massive rock—which had borne one corpse when I departed Hazelfeur—is laden with mauled bodies. Crows brave the haze of heat emanating from the stone, dipping to snap bits of flesh up in their beaks, never landing out of respect for the dead.

"Oh my gods," I gasp, dread building as I squint, searching for Nathaire among the mass of sun-browned corpses.

My gorge rises when I see the tiny, slender fingers that

held my hands as we danced for the Dagda and combed through my hair only nights ago, though where they had been pink with youth then, they're now pale with death.

Teniélín, one of Onora's brood.

I choke on bile, feeling as if I could keel over and never get up, but a fleshbear rolls into my vision like a tidal wave. Without hesitation I harness the tightness in my gut, molding it into steel, forging forward with not just my blade's fury but my own. I sling Thornfury low, flicking sharply so his curved tip hooks cruelly into the back of the bear's foreleg and then flicking again to pull his blade back toward me—through the leg.

The bear heaves forward with a grating groan, leg buckling and yet still uncowed.

Steel blazes hot behind my eyes. I snap Thornfury's chain again, carving through the bear's other foreleg.

The bear collapses, sufficiently crippled, but before I can so much as fathom a sense of vicious triumph, an arrow fletched with emerald feathers lances through the beast's eye socket.

The bear stills, feeling pain no more.

"It deserved worse," I say as Nathaire trots into the clearing.

He frowns, swiping sweat and blood from his brow. His fingers flash. *"Your eyebrows are gone,"* he signs.

"Pulled them out, I guess." I shrug, feeling suddenly heavy. A sharp pain flares where the wraithbear struck me, and I clutch my side with a wince.

"I packed you goldroot."

Even if I had words, they wouldn't come.

In Nathaire's presence, I feel too much—relief that he's alive, desperation at Hazelfeur's falling, grief for Onora's loss, anger that I'm unable to do what I swore to do. And that ever-present unraveling, the threads holding me together fraying with every too-short breath.

Nathaire waves a hand close to my face, then grips my shoulders as I sway, pressing his thumbs into my jaw so I have to look at him. Though his forehead strains with worry and his eyes convey apology, he shakes his head.

He takes his hands away to sign, *"Tell it to the bees,"* then unclasps the bone rose at the peak of my sternum and pushes my pelts off my neck. They thump to the dirt at my heels. *"There are more bears. Do not fall apart yet."*

And then he leads me, of all places, to the púca's temple.

When we were young and culturing waywardness, Nathaire and I sought to steal a look inside the púca's temple. We had never been forbidden from doing so, but the elders discouraged interaction with the sprites in fear that they would swindle Hazelfeur out of more than the shares required by the Pact.

However, we had no interest in speaking with the púca—we harbored a healthy wariness of the gaunt-limbed, molten-eyed monsters, and only wished to discover what secrets their sanctuary hid.

And so I devised a distraction in the form of a pesky pie-bald cat who had ransacked meat stores, terrorized the chickens, and torn holes in the wattle-and-daub siding of over half the roundhouses in the village. Though it scream-ed murder, I snagged the mangy terror by its scruff and marched it up to the púca's temple at moonswake while Nathaire waited in the shadows, his honey-crystal eyes gleaming from beneath the low eaves.

An owlish púca appeared with a sound like dry leaves shuffling, its wide head cocking at the yowling cat. No ex-pression crossed its face, but I could tell it was annoyed by the slight bristle of oily feathers fringing its neck.

I waggled the cat at arm's length, and behind the púca, I saw Nathaire slip past the temple's weathered tapestry.

"The harvest is inside it," I said of the cat. "Ate the only egg the chickens gave. So...here."

The púca clacked its beak, and bristly down rippled under its jaw. "What need have we for a cat? Its patchy hide would hardly make an interesting covering for a moldering melon." Another clack of its beak. "What use have we for a cat, girl child?"

"It sort of sings, if you plug your ears just right. Underwater. After drowning." I waggled the cat again.

"No gratitudes."

"I can carry it inside for you, if you'd like."

Nathaire emerged from under the tapestry and darted back into the shadows, and I dropped the cat. It skittered between the púca's verrucous legs and clawed its way up the tapestry, screeching all the while.

And then I took my hasty leave, racing after Nathaire toward the lean-to we would hide in when the elders were feeling particularly preachy, and which otherwise was the property of the one-eyed goat. I ducked inside, giggling despite the racing of my heart, and gave the goat's chin a tickle before huddling close to Nathaire.

"What was in there?" I asked, searching his face for a hint of what he found. "Was it horrible? Smelly? Were they sleeping on the ceiling, or spinning their heads on sticks?"

Nathaire lifted his foot, revealing a coating of wet muck.

"Crows." I sniffed tentatively. "Is that blood—is that what they bleed?"

His fingers twitched, uncertain. "*It was a lake,*" he finally signed.

"A lake? What was a lake? A lake of blood?"

He shook his head. "*Inside the temple, a lake. Caves up high.*" A pause, then he brought his knuckles together. "*How?*"

I didn't have an answer.

Outside of the púca's temple, I curl my fingers into my threadbare trousers, tugging the fabric away from my thighs in quick, nervous jerks. I pluck up a ribbon of tall grass and strip it apart. Then another, and another.

Nathaire picks up the frayed bits as I drop them, juggling the snarled beads of grass in his palm until the wind claims them, sweeping my worries up to the careless gods.

"There will be more bears," he signs after a time, pointing toward Bairnhart Forest. *"More and more and more."*

I swallow hard, thinking of the Dagda's tale, of the woman and child he lost so odiously. "I learned something, Nathaire. About the púca. They fought against this village once before, killed its people in favor of their god. In favor of Artio's *father*. I cannot..." Another golden-tipped blade of grass falls prey to my restless fingers. "I cannot trust them. Not with my people."

"I also learned things about the púca." Nathaire's movements are fluid, free of hesitation, but a shadow crossing his face robs the words of subtlety. I realize how tired he looks, black smudges bruised beneath his eyes.

"What did you learn?" I press, whole chunks of grass

riving apart under my frantically tearing fingers. "Nathaire, I asked you to protect—"

"*Come inside*," he signs, walking backward toward the moldering tapestry. The convergence of his form against its imagery jars me for a moment—golden eyes, dark hair, twisted tongues.

He follows my gaze, then turns back to me. The shadow again flits across his face; calcifies in his eyes; draws his mouth into an uneasy rictus.

"*Come inside, Roz,*" he signs again, and holds out his hand.

I take it.

We go inside.

The first thing I notice inside the temple is that—though outside the roof is lathed with sooty daub and capped by the towering finial horns—there is no ceiling, only a ring of thorny spires far above and a stream of drowsy sunlight filtering down to set aglow the muddy morass that stretches far wider than it logically should.

A lake, brown-watered with shores cluttered by hard-earned harvests—detritus of the Pact, I realize with no dearth of resentment—just as Nathaire insisted all those equinoxes ago.

And surrounding the lake, set into the high walls with no apparent way to get to them but for the caul of moss laced over the stone, small notches of indeterminable depth. Caves, dozens of them. Nests, perhaps?

All of it should be impossible, but I hardly ogle—it's the púca's residence, after all, and more prevalent is my concern for the people of Hazelfeur who mill about the discolored lake. Despite the eerie radiance of the temple, there is a thick, viscous pall of grief that clogs the air, unseen but no less heavy.

I seize Nathaire's arm for support as the fullness of

Hazelfeur's hurt washes over me.

I can *see* it. I can see that it wasn't a hole that grief carved into my people—no, it hadn't taken anything away at all. They weren't hollowed out by all the sorrow and all the rage but rather filled with it, packed like hard snow until their insides were swollen with black wrath.

I can see that in the past days they've grown fuller with turmoil. I see it in the lines of their faces and the hunch of their shoulders, in the way that they breathe and walk and talk; tight, quiet, ghostlike, as if they're afraid of bursting.

They have lost so much.

When they look at me, it is with neither relief nor disappointment, and I feel the heaviness of that, too. In my absence, they decided it wasn't worth expecting anything upon my return, any faith they once had for me gone in a blaze of bear jaws and wraith claws. In my absence they stopped thinking of me as Bearslayer—perhaps even stopped thinking of me altogether—and they would be right not to. I was not here to slay bears, as I swore to do.

"I swore," I whisper, shaken beyond reaction, numb to the stifled sobs bouncing off the water, numb to the bloodstained bandages and fevered brows, numb to the hooded eyes watching from the alcoves overhead, numb even to the ache of my cracked ribs.

Nathaire signs something close to his chest, but I cannot tear my gaze from the breadth of hurt I inflicted by abandoning Hazelfeur.

I finally find Onora—who is usually easy to spot with

her colorful glass hair beads and paint-covered skin—and her grief is the worst of all. It is visible on her skin. It has already desolated her brightness, razed away her serenity, laid waste to everything that made her Onora.

Seeing her makes me selfish; I consider falling to pieces, giving in to that which threatens to undo me.

But my failures are nothing—not now, not here.

I shuck free of my self-pity, shrugging it off like I did my furs. Off to the bees.

Then I rush across the temple to where Onora tends injured villagers, my feet slapping in the spongy mire. I see my past harvests sunk into the lake's shore: rabbits' feet, goat horns, tulsi berry husks, sprigs of bearsbane. All discarded, forgotten to waste, likely laughed over by the wily host of púca.

I come upon Onora and fall to my knees beside her, watching her usually steady hands tremble furiously over a man's near-severed arm. I touch her elbow, choking back tears at the sight of her unadorned, unkempt hair and the dark streaks of mourning in place of her typical brightness.

She jerks back, wheeling away from me, her face a contortion of unbated fury, her eyes the hellish blaze of an untamed fire.

My lungs seize as if transpierced by spurs of broken bone. "Onora, I—"

Her hand falls heavy against my cheek.

As blurry black worms swim across my vision, Onora's voice rises in a wordless, daggering keen. Then my head clears of the blow and I see her curled against the ground, white fingers pressed against her mouth, overwhelmed by her loss. Broken—perhaps irreparably.

*E*ver since Onora took to watching over me in the ways I imagined a mother would—tutting over my perpetual filthiness, sewing up my wounds, offering her hearth to make me feel less alone, less *other*—I never stopped to wonder why she paid me such tender devotion, nor did I wonder what I would be without it.

There was hope before. A tiny flicker against the wind, one which illuminated a possibility of family, of belonging. Of a mother.

But that was before.

With goldroot tea seemingly magicked from the air in hand, Nathaire draws me away from Onora and leads me to a boggy edge of the lake. The foul water and littered harvests do nothing to soothe me.

"*Tears need their time to pass,*" Nathaire signs, having set the bowl of tea on a stone festooned with lichen. He moves to block the rest of the temple from my view. "*All of it needs time. There will be waves. And they will rise and accept their warrior spirits, much like you.*"

I frown. "Why are you talking like that?"

He doesn't meet my eyes, and it is unlike Nathaire to withhold things from me.

"Nathaire, what did you learn?" I demand, grateful for the curiosity dissuading my mind from the pitch of desperation. "Why are we *here*, in this temple, while our home falls to ruin outside?"

His throat bobs as he swallows, and when he takes my hand I can feel the uncertain flutter of his pulse. With his free hand he makes a gesture: "*Calm.*" Then he guides my hand to the crown of his head.

Through his coarse, ember-dark curls I feel something—a raised knot of what feels like exposed skull.

I gasp and snatch my hand away. "You're hurt! You goathead, why haven't you—"

Nathaire shakes his head and grabs my hand, again pressing it to the protrusion, again signing with one hand. *"Calm. Feel."*

"What, you want me to feel how dense you are?" I tease through gritted teeth. "Trust me, I am well familiar..." I trail off as my fingers explore the lump.

It is bone, but not the bone of his skull. It is rougher, scalier, like the young bark of a tree's new growth, and around the base, a mound of puckered tissue rises from his scalp. Scarcely breathing, I comb through the hair on the other side of his head and find another growth there, slightly smaller but no less disconcerting.

"Crows," I gasp, tearing out strands of his hair as I rip my hand away. "You've got horns."

Nathaire's lips flatten, straining against a wary tremble. *"Goathead indeed,"* he signs, a jest I'm too shocked to appreciate.

"Crows," I say again, my jaw quivering dumbly.

"Please be calm, Roz. I have only just found out."

"That you have horns? By the godsdamned *crows*, Nathaire, I thought you combed your hair more often than I." I struggle to keep my voice down as my mind whirls with the implications of his horns. Then my stomach turns. "You said...you said this has to do with the púca."

His hands remain still as stone.

"Nathaire."

"The old god you spoke of." A pause. *"The púca's god."*

I squeeze my fingertips. "What of him?"

"They call him the horned one." Another pause, longer this time. *"The god of rebirth."*

"Nathaire," I say again, the imminent revelation a loud bloodrush in my ears. "Speak plainly."

He winces, then glances over his shoulder. Behind him, two púca spawn like unholy centrinels.

I startle, my foot splashing in the lake's shallows, mud sucking hungrily at my heel.

"Calm," Nathaire signs.

"Stop saying that," I snap. Though it's warm inside the temple, I shiver, my muscles locked into bands of icy steel.

The púca on the left—a shrew-faced demon with one too many joints in its goosefleshed arms—clucks a purple tongue. "Greetings, Bearslayer. Much has found light in your absence. Don't you think it strange?"

"Strange, indeed, warrior rose," says the other púca, an ugly reptilian beast. "It is what you don't wish to know that is now all you know. Strange indeed."

"Nathaire," I hiss, snapping my thumb against my knuckles, each snap of pain grounding me, "what in Morrigan's blackened throat is the meaning of this?"

Nathaire's fingers flash like lightning, his face the storm behind it. *"I am the horned one—the old one—the wild one. I am Cernunnos reborn."*

I remember a time before Nathaire learned to speak with his hands, a time when we hadn't yet forged friendship for lack of a means to communicate.

He and I and another orphan, Caoimhe—who prayed to Áine for beauty almost as often as she breathed—lived among the elders, cycled through their homes to allow them reprieve from the two of us they didn't favor. From the two of us who failed to amuse them with prayers and normal Hazelfeur dreams; dreams of child-rearing and sheep-rearing and reverence-rearing.

Nathaire was the first to rebel. He would escape from Èilde Malvynn or Èilde Saibh or Èilde Diarmuid, whoever cared for him that moon, and would slip off into the scrublands at sunswake.

I would watch him go, feeling a strange fragmenting within myself—a breaking apart of the fear that I couldn't be free of the set ways of the village; of the fear that if I wandered, I would never belong.

Watching Nathaire dash through the heather, his body a curved bronze arrow, I started to wonder.

I wondered if being wild was like power to him; if being wild was the comfort to him that religion and sameness was to the elders.

I wondered if being wild was what he really and truly *knew*; if being wild was his forever.

His unflinching inclination toward freedom made me wonder if being wild could be my forever, too.

athaire waits for me to speak, but his expectations of a reply are for naught. I make an unintelligible sound and turn to retch into the púca's pool, feeling some amount of shame—but not remorse—as I do.

Diomath is Artio's daughter.

Nathaire is Cernunnos reborn.

And I... I am something. I hardly know if it's worth finding out what.

In this moment, though, I am a poor friend, and I flee the temple.

I know Nathaire—*the horned one*—will understand, but I can't bear to look at him, to see the dismay in his eyes. Nor can I bear to be so near Onora's grief, the grief she blames me for. The grief I caused.

I tear out of the temple with a hoarse scream, thinking it impossible Nathaire could be wilder than I as I run full-footed through a village empty of villagers. It is not the Hazelfeur I know, not without its people—not with so many of them dead.

I have come back to so many things I cannot bear to see.

Things which I now run from, among them my failures as Bearslayer.

I only wield Thornfury for his familiarity and for the protection he offers, and I steer clear of Artio's spawn, dispelling any instinctual recklessness that interrupts the single pursuit which guides my feet: *enchantress.*

Spring-bright eyes and rosebud lips.

Cloud-white cheeks pearling with a smile.

That untouchable, fluttering feeling.

Unfulfilled longing, allure.

I leave Hazelfeur behind in distance and in mind, and soon I come to the clearing of trees where I first saw her.

Was it only days ago? It feels like moons, far too many moons. Each one a dream of her.

"*Dìomath,*" I whisper, a sweetness on my tongue.

"Rhoswen."

And she is there, and she is in my arms, and I am lost to her.

he holds secrets under her skin.

Secrets and stars.

iomath feeds me golden apples, crisp with ripeness, and slips swollen bilberries between my lips. Her face is mottled by rays of sunlight, a most brilliant mosaic I can't seem to behold fully enough, and her words are tantalizing as hope. I feel as if I've drunk a riverful of goldroot tea.

She finds the soreness in my side, settling her palm over the ache in my ribs—a quick sting—and then kisses me—and all the pain abates. Her smile warms me, chases the bitter vestiges of disquietude from my chest.

"Your resilience is no small thing," she says—cloying, tantalizing words I wouldn't believe from any other's lips.

"I wish to be anything but resilient." I sigh heavily, watching her eyelashes flutter with my breath. She is so close. "I'm exhausted by feigning this...this *strength*. It's such a human thing of me, isn't it? To pretend to be strong? I'm sick of being human, Dìomath. I'm sick of proving my worth."

She tilts her head, and what remains of winter's color falls away beneath her shadow. "Whose respect do you seek?" she asks. Her fingers set my skin athrill and affect liquid warmth along my collarbone.

"Anyone who will give it," I reply uncertainly.

"You're something of an impossibility, aren't you, my rose? An impossible woman. But you don't know that." She touches my hair, winds it gently free of my hasty knots. "Your devotion to duty brings you pain. It always has, hasn't it?"

The admission of my weakness makes me feel vulnerable, more vulnerable even than my bare skin. I bite my lip but she leans forward to kiss it, coaxing it away from my teeth and soothing the sting.

"This despairing pain of yours," she whispers, "is how you know who you are. It is how you know what matters, so even this pain can be seen as a gift. Your people know what you're made of, and I know what you're made of—wildflowers, wildfires, and the stars still shining at sunswake. But this pain, it's an opportunity for *you* to know what you're made of. An opportunity to earn your own respect."

I stare at her, unable to find words as eloquent as she. "Wildflowers and wildfires..."

"And freckles," she laughs. "So many freckles."

And she kisses every one.

My guilt returns with the sun's descent, and the lingering taste of apples turns sour on my tongue. I had thought remaining with Dìomath under the trees' solicitous patchwork canopy would save me from thoughts of Hazelfeur, of Onora, of Teniélín, of Nathaire, of gods and their sons and descendants and reincarnations—but my despair refuses to be so easily shaken. The impresence of chaos still does not mean peace.

Between my enchantress's calming nature and Bairnhart's quieting susurrus, somehow I've let myself forget what this place is and to whom it belongs. I've forgotten that to Dìomath, this place is a prison.

Fearing that my journey's failure would bring her anguish, I delayed telling her of what happened on the Dagda's mountain, but now I rise from the forest floor, drawing her up with me. I squeeze her hands so she doesn't feel mine tremble.

"Dìomath, you must know I did not come bearing good tidings. Your—your bear, he turned on the Dagda's sons, and—"

She shakes her head, eyes flashing not with shock but with something more honest, more righteous. "We do not need *him*," she spits, "or his bastard sons. Éamon did no more than I would have."

"That cannot possibly be true," I murmur, surprised at the scathing in her voice. "And the harp...she must be played by the blood of Dagda. She won't respond to anyone else. All hope of wielding her power against your mother is lost. I wish it weren't so, you must know that, but I will stop at nothing to end Artio's reign. I only need your help—"

"I cannot find her for you. It's not the way, Rhoswen." She pulls me closer, resting her forearms against my sternum, and I notice the wetness glinting along her eyelashes.

My throat constricts, my heart torn between what she is asking of me and what I feel for her. But I know the wholeness of my heart is with her, not with her mother's death. It will always be with her.

I nod.

"You *found* the harp, though, did you not?" Dìomath asks. "Did you bring her with you?"

"I brought her to Hazelfeur, yes, but—"

"You haven't touched her strings? You haven't played her?"

I shake my head as I step back, away from the eagerness in her voice which overwhelms me with shame. "It would be for naught, Dìomath. She won't respond to me."

"Have you tried, though?" she presses.

"No, I—"

"Have you plucked even one string with intent—with pure and true intent?"

"It would be foolish to even try! She is not *made* for me, don't you understand? I'm not—not *worthy*, or some goatshit nonsense. It doesn't matter. I can't play her, Dìomath. I can't free you from these woods."

I wait for the too-bright hope in her gaze to peter out, but it doesn't diminish. She only grasps my wrists. "It has nothing to do with your worth. Ràithne will sing for you."

She lifts onto her toes to rest her forehead against mine, and she smells of sweet earth and freshly melted snow. "Go. Make her sing for me, my rose."

Her voice is my intoxication; her word is my command.

$\mathcal{T}$he village is quiet upon my return, my people still holed up within the púca's temple, Artio's spawn seeming to have retreated for a time and the crows having had their fill of death.

I don't startle when a form drops down from the horns of the temple as I pass it by; Nathaire falls silently into step with me, bow in hand.

We pass the ruins of Èilde Malvynn's hut and I ask, "Is he...?"

"*Dead*," Nathaire signs. He carefully picks through the refuse, stopping to pocket the carved stag I earlier trod on before returning to my side.

"What of Saibh?"

He shakes his head. "*Nor Diarmuid. All the elders are dead.*"

I press my teeth together so tightly my jaw pops, and the hurt reminds me of Dìomath's words.

A gift, this pain.

"Do you have recollections of your previous life?" I ask Nathaire—an acknowledgment, an apology.

He snorts, slinging his bow across his back to free his hands. *"Lives,"* he corrects me. *"I recall...sensations. Feelings of having been places and known people. Mostly I remember death."*

"Is it horrible?"

"No," he signs, then considers for a moment. *"It is not much of anything."*

"That's not very poetic," I say, pulling an overdrawn frown. "I was expecting you to wax on about how freeing or transformative or sacred it is. I expected the word *ether* at least once. Isn't anything, aye?"

He rolls his eyes. *"It is not nothing, but becoming nothing...what else could it be?"*

"I've not died before, Natty. But I'd say it smells."

"You think everything smells, Roz."

"It's true. But nothing more than you."

He gasps in mock offense, swiping my arm with his knuckles, and for a moment everything could be normal—we could be setting out to hunt hares in the scrublands, ankles wrapped to protect against piskie bites, Nathaire humming even as I complain that it hurts my ears. We could later return to drop off a portion of our game at the púca's temple, me muttering obscenities as we scurry away only to be scolded for my foul mouth and sent to the hawthorn tree, where Èilde Malvynn would beseech me to use my tongue to pray rather than curse, and Nathaire would taunt me with his silence, which never got him in trouble. We could lay our heads on my furs at moonswake and throw bear teeth into the hearth, and I could have my moments of panic, after which Nathaire would poke fun at my swollen face and then kiss the tears away.

Certainly our lives were never normal, not for a boy with two tongues and a girl born to fight bears, but there was something to our life that once seemed tame.

Perhaps we just grew older, and the darkness could hide no longer.

Or perhaps the gods just deigned to interfere.

I abruptly stop walking and crush myself into Nathaire, hugging him fiercely.

"I would be a lousy god, lousy as the rest of them," I say in a rush, "but you could be a good one, Nathaire. You could be the best of the gods, no matter what you've done in past lives. You don't have to be him—that's why they call him the old god, aye? Be whatever you want to be. Just... don't get so friendly with the púca. They might worship you, but they're an ugly lot. No one will warm your bed if you reek of that lake, mind you. I wouldn't."

Nathaire's chest thrums with laughter. He embraces me tightly, then pulls back. *"I must be off to take a long swim, then. Farewell, you smelly not-god,"* he signs, then waves and turns as if to walk away. I grab his wrist, both of us snickering.

"Don't go," I say, the laughter imbuing me with a sudden need for honesty. "I have to tell you something, and it may come as a shock, but you have a granddaughter. And I care for her—it seems important you know."

His grin falters. *"I think I would remember if I had a granddaughter."*

"You banished Artio to the forest, or so says the Dagda. You likely wouldn't have known she had a daughter, but—"

"*You don't think I would have known?*"

"If you were as oblivious then as you are in this life, you wouldn't have." I shrug, somewhat disappointed by his reaction but no less deterred. "But the girl—your granddaughter—her name is Dìomath. And she is..."

Beautiful, radiant, a rapture.

But Nathaire isn't listening. He blinks rapidly and his brows dip close to the bridge of his nose, deep in thought.

"It looks painful, having centuries of memories," I mutter, then I leave him to his harkening-back and stride several paces away to where I left Ràithne, hope's harbinger.

I stand the harp up in the grass and pluck a flowered clover free from her strings. Crouching before her, wilted crescent-moon petals disintegrating in my fist, I squint at the smooth stones inlaid in the wood of the harp, wishing she would give some sign or sound to save me from this moment.

I hear Nathaire come up behind me. He circles to the other side of Ràithne and gives me a questioning look. *"What are you doing?"*

"I'm afraid," I admit.

The harp doesn't speak.

Nathaire squats, inspecting Ràithne for whatever threat she supposedly poses. He again gives me a look.

"Only blood of the Dagda can play her," I say, jamming my thumbnail between my front teeth. "And I'm afraid."

"Afraid to try?" he asks, and when I nod he flicks a string. Strangely, and though the horsehair shivers, the harp makes no noise. He then lightly drags his fingertips across a dozen of the strings.

Ràithne remains mute.

"*No Dagda blood in me,*" Nathaire signs. "*Bless Aengus's filthy toenails.*"

"I could've told you that, you dozy turnip. Artio and the Dagda had *relations*, so were you to be kin to the Dagda, that would be a right scandal, aye? Though I suppose incest could mean nothing to the gods—I hardly know what goes, you know I never paid the elders much mind." The words sober me, quickly putting an end to my blathering, and my thumbnail slices upward into my gums. I snatch my hand away from my mouth, but still can't seem to breach the space between my fingers and the unforthcoming harp. "Nathaire, I...it's not entirely impossible that I have his blood. The Dagda's."

Nathaire leans back on his heels and waits for me to go on.

"He lived here, in Hazelfeur, for a short time. He was here to put an end to Cernunnos's—ah, to *your* rule, actually." I run my hand up my arm and pinch the tender skin inside the crease of my elbow, my blood buzzing with nervous energy. I frown at the globes of white clover in the grass, wondering how long it would take to deplume each one of its petals; how long it would distract me from the statue of the strong-jawed stone woman in the Dagda's hall. "He kept the company of a villager. Close company."

Face schooled into an expression of placid interest, Nathaire's understanding manifests only in the twitch of his brow. "*You think it could have been your mother.*"

My eyes grow hot and a strangled noise escapes me as I

attempt to push down the seething mass of uncertainties roiling in my gut. "She *could* have been, but she died. She was murdered with the child yet unborn. The Dagda found her with...with her womb carved out of her. The child would have died, then—wouldn't it have died?"

Nathaire gets up and moves to my side, resting a hand on my arm to protect the wisps of hair there from my hawkishly plucking fingers.

"It does not have to mean anything, if it is true," he signs, his movements fierce. *"We can be whatever we want to be, remember?"*

"You're a god, and death isn't anything to you," I say, and my words are sharp teeth. "But it would be to me—as would this. I would have the death of a mother to mourn, and a drunkard father who left this village to burn. That's not nothing, is it?"

"We put too much weight on godhood, Roz. We have not been fair."

"You would say that—"

He pounds his palm with his fist to interrupt me. *"And you should understand it better than anyone! To feel every choice and to feel the consequence of each upon a whole people, is that not what you expect of a god? Is that not what you expect of yourself, Bearslayer? You have given a lifetime, and look at you. You are tired, and I am tired, and isn't that enough? Flesh and bones have their limits. To call something god..."* A pause, heavy with an abrasive awareness. *"It is just a name. It is nothing without respect."*

My hands fall still in my lap, and I recall the Dagda as he told his tragic tale. He was nothing more than a grieving man, and I had pity for him, just as I have pity for Onora. I would not blame Onora for leaving Hazelfeur, for wouldn't it remind her of all she has lost?

I grasp Nathaire's hand, nodding my appreciation for his words. My chest too tight to speak fully, I whisper, "I'm still afraid."

But fear is only worsened by inaction, and so I face it head-on, fingers outstretched.

At first, there is no sound.

I feel the twisted strands of horsehair like a whip against the pad of my forefinger, the string's coarseness scraping against the soft callus in a manner not unlike Thornfury's blade carving through wraith bones.

I close my eyes as my fingertip drops from one string to the next, holding my breath, truly unable to hear over the bloodrush in my ears. Each beat of my heart is an eternal peal of thunder, and lightning prickles beneath my skin.

Then...a sound.

A sound for only me.

The sound, I know—in some fathomless recess of my mind—is Ràithne's song, called forth by my touch. But it doesn't feel like noise; doesn't sound like any music I've heard before.

No, the sound is a feeling.

It is my soul made tangible, a deep ocean of emotion conjured in each note.

It is a voice I didn't know I had access to, one of truth and shameless asking.

It is an invitation to breathe, and a contentment with slowness I've never known.

It is an ode to nature—to *my* nature.

A sound unfathomable.

A shifting of the stars.

I gasp and break the union between Ràithne and me, the wave of *feeling* lingering like the sweet burn of tulsi wine, and for a moment I do what she asked of me: I breathe.

I look to Nathaire, and he seems as breathless as I, and almost as fearful. His hands hover, outstretched, prepared to either draw an arrow or grasp my shoulders—to push my pelts off, I realize. An instinctual response to calm me.

But, strange and unheard of as it is, I find myself needing no calming, even as the residue of Ràithne's song thrums in my bones.

"Danu's heaving tits," I wheeze, feeling much like the wildfire Dìomath said I was made of.

Nathaire looks utterly terrified. "*You—*"

But I grab his arms and shake him, my every nerve alight with disbelief. "Forget the Dagda, Natty! Spring can be forgone...Hazelfeur can be saved!"

And my enchantress can be freed.

I spring to my feet, the clammy burden and hopelessness of the past days absolved of their command over me. I try not to dwell on how easily the weight lifted, one moment suffocating me and the next gone; a long-settled coat of dust finally shaken free.

Lifting Ràithne carefully, I hurry to the old stone wall outside the village, stalks of heather feathersoft beneath my feet. I sit on the stones and set Ràithne on the ground between my knees, settling the lower of the wood's twin arches against my shoulder.

The mossy pearlwort that has overtaken the low wall tickles my arms. I lightly touch the clusters of its buds, brushing my palm over the tiny green pearls. I offer a silent promise to nurture their growth with the harp's power.

Pure and true intent.

Ràithne's strings hum eagerly under my touch, and this time the sound is a warm greeting, a comfort, a bond. I don't need to speak, nor ask, nor command—she understands what I seek, my meaning conveyed through the heat of my flesh, each ridge of my fingerprint gravid with fervor.

Spring must pass, I sing.

And though perhaps she was built for my blood, Ràithne is a friend, and she asks for nothing in return but my company, and the music is not her song but *ours*. We're lost to it as a mother would be to her child, intimately and boundlessly, together contriving an unseen fabric and weaving it into the passage of time, nurturing the present into something else.

Should it feel unnatural, this changing of the known? It doesn't, nor does it feel like I made the choice to bring it about.

Spring will pass, we sing.

In the haze of sound and not-sound and the distorted light of sunsleep, I perceive the change in my periphery: the pearlwort buds fragmenting, tufted petals unfurling delicately, inchoate blooms responding to our song. And beyond that, the smear of clouds unmasks the sky, clearing the way for their fiery queen to slash low against the scrublands, haloing formations of rocks fuzzed over with fulcress and squill.

Time stretches, and the yellow catkins of the hazelnut trees recede into the bright greenery bursting forth, bright crimson flowers pollinated and hoping to fruit with the earth's warming. Tulsi berries grow fat and dark on scraggly shrubs that can scarcely hold their weight, and the fragrance of their vitality draws brown-ruffed grouse from piles of brush. The din of insects wavers fitfully, but it is not unpleasant, rather serving to mark the crescendo of the changing; to punctuate it.

Spring has come and gone, and our song has summered the earth.

𝕴 feel as if I've climbed a mountain to its summit, or perhaps sunk to the very bottom of the sea. As I lean away from Ràithne, my lungs don't quite know what to make of the feeling, nor do my limbs.

Am I a spent vessel, or a full one?

I sit heavy on the wall, faced with the breadth of late summer, my sweat already evaporated into the dry air. I hear my breath as if through a tunnel. My scalp prickles, and my thoughts grow sticky with a pleasant drone, like that of sleepy bees, my mind devolving into a lazy, honey-sick hive.

A figure comes into view, a dark silhouette ringed by a nimbus of light. Its hands move, and I recognize it as voiceless speech, but after the season-effecting and the discovery of life's ephemerality and time's sudden malleability... words seem vastly insignificant.

What seems most important now is sleep, and with little warning, my body succumbs to its pull.

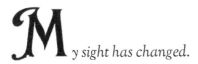y sight has changed.

I am sure, at first, I must be seeing through the eyes of a bird.

I am looking down upon a black-cradled ground, a fluid stretch of plain, nary a beast to be found.

I do not feel like a bird.

There is no freedom in this sight, only a certainty that I have a self, and abilities, though for what use is not clear.

So, too, do I know there is no one to guide me, even were I to ask the stars.

They would laugh.

The field's grasses are strange from here, smooth. Not one grass nor many, but an ocean, an entity.

But no—here and there one stalk rises above the rest, distinct and golden-tipped, ridges and flaws suddenly visible, a singular

243

marvel and then gone again.

I reach out to touch them, but the ocean shifts and recoils, afraid, and even I am wary of myself now—I am not like them—the one, the all.

Then, awareness of the perspective from which I contemplate the field: I am not above, nor below, nor among.

I don't know what I am.

I don't know what I am for.

I wake disoriented, my hand grasping for Thornfury before I even comprehend where I am. Finding him safely sheathed at my hip and with no apparent need to use him, I grapple first with the unfamiliar sensation of having slept too long, and then with the saccharine smell of goldroot tea—together, the two render me roundly wooly-headed.

I sit up, the heels of my hands pushing into the dense, coarse furs of my sleeping pallet. I vigorously knead my knuckles into my eyes, then squint to see in the dim of my roundhouse. Ràithne graces my perception first, her simple elegance less out of place than I would have imagined against the shoddily patched walls. Bowls sit over the low fire in various states of steeping, drying bunches of goldroot noosed from the thatch above.

Nathaire, of course, ever-present as he is, crouches over a partially-skinned badger near the hearth. Where usually he works the skin off his game with practiced efficiency, he now seems to be taking his time, reverence in the restraint of his muscles.

"You can hardly hurt it, you know," I say, my voice

husky with sleep. "You needn't be so maiden-fingered with it."

Nathaire looks up, hair hanging in his eyes, brow crested in concern. "*You slept. I was worried you would not wake.*"

"You weren't...praying to it, were you? The badger?"

"*I took life to restore life.*" He wipes his hands on a bloodied cloth, then touches a cord around his neck—a new pendant, though bulging beneath his tunic it looks too big to be Èilde Malvynn's carved stag. "*It has new meaning.*"

I sigh, rubbing my eyes again, too foggy to ask after his necklace. "Doesn't everything?"

Nathaire nods, neatly folds away his tools, then hurries to pour a bowl of tea.

"I can't stand the smell of it, Nathaire," I say to stop him. I stand, my bones stiff with sluggishness, and move toward the doorway through which early sunswake gleams flatly.

I slept a full night. No wonder Nathaire thought I wouldn't wake.

At the revelation, I snap around to look at the badger. "Where did you—did you hunt that today?"

Mischief dusts the apples of his cheeks pink as his head wags side to side. "*No, I hunted it several moons past.*"

"Nathaire."

He leaves the hearth and takes my elbow, leading me outside. Stretching his arms wide, he looks for all the world like a child who's just witnessed sunswake for the first time.

"*Not a bear to be beheld,*" he signs. "*Not last night, not*

246

this morn. They sleep, Roz. All of them. Spring has gone."

My jaw shifts, my mouth working before my voice can. "Where did you hunt the badger? Tell me, you goathead, or I'll shove your horns where the sun—"

"*Bairnhart.*"

"And the bears there, were they...?" I still don't dare hope.

Nathaire's lips pull to the side. He nods. "*Asleep.*"

"You saw them?"

"*Some did not even make it to their den.*"

My hands go to my mouth, palms pressed flat against my lips to keep my heart from disgorging itself from my body. My insides seem to puddle into a mass of burning, feathering oil. It feels as if I've swallowed a will-o'-the-wisp.

The bears sleep.

I am not sure what it means for me.

As the people of Hazelfeur tentatively emerge from the púca's temple, each step they take laden with a confusion of relief and grief, I wonder at my enchantress. I worry for my village, and for the path to restoring our homes and stores and hearts, but so, too, do I worry for Dìomath. Where I know Hazelfeur is safe from Artio, I cannot assume the same of Dìomath, and it is a particularly insistent thought—that she may yet still be in danger.

Onora also weighs on my mind, but she seems to have found a semblance of peace in her healing work, and the magnitude of injuries my people sustained will likely keep her busy for days to come. Nathaire told me to give her tears time to pass, though I wonder if it's not something deeper that needs the time, something less easily wiped away—if ever.

I worry our *before* wasn't enough to salvage what has come to pass.

I itch with all the worry, my fingers restless and scouring my arms for scabs, my hips aching when I fail to move my legs. I had expected the anxiety to pass with the passing of spring, but the well of unease seems only to have deepened. It is a new world without the bears.

When I ask Nathaire if he happened upon Dìomath in Bairnhart, he says he saw nothing but sleeping bears and summer-boldened creatures, and he shows no interest in entertaining my worries. With goldroot clouding his eyes, his attention is absorbed fully by the dead badger—which he takes an inordinate amount of time attending to—and whatever thoughts of deityhood plague his mind.

And so I turn to my mantle of bear pelts, still splayed on the ground in the crook of the village. At a glance, lying among the bearspawn I felled yesterday, it could simply be another corpse. It's dirtied enough, for certain; I neglected to keep it clean beyond its first oiling.

I pick up the heavy furs, marveling for a moment that I ever kept such weight upon my neck. I am older and stronger than when I first donned them, and yet they've only grown more wearying with each passing equinox. Now they seem an unbearable onus.

I decide to leave them with the corpses, rose brooch and all.

It is a different feeling walking into Bairnhart Forest knowing I will not be disturbed by Artio's spawn despite the absence of snow.

Winter always comes quietly upon Bairnhart, and must be taken advantage of before Artio wakes. Usually, Nathaire and I hunt in the scrublands or the shallow woods until the hibernal solstice, and only when the trees are sheathed to their bellies in ice do we assail the forest to stalk its foxes and elk. We have little regard for stealth while our enemies hibernate—Nathaire has often found the niveous landscape an ideal haven in which to dispel his wordless voice; in which the snow is happy to swallow the limitations of his malformed tongues.

In Bairnhart's winter, we scream.

Outside of winter, though, any time I've found my feet in these woods, so too has Thornfury found his blade in bear blood.

And so, though Ràithne and I put Artio's reign to rest, I wield my scythe. Disbelief still threads my muscles with strain, even as I come upon an unmoving mass of fleshbear:

not dead, only sleeping. Its ribs rise almost imperceptibly, like slow-growing tumors.

"Oi," I say, toeing one of its legs roughly. "Say nothing if you agree that you're an arse-licking bastard."

The bear slumbers on.

"Crows. You truly are asleep..."

I marvel at the sight a breath longer and then move on, the strain relinquishing some as I run toward Dìomath's hollow, passing an inert wraithbear—eerier even in sleep than awake—and another, and another, and another.

It was as Nathaire said. They all sleep.

Without breaking stride, I drop into the hole in the ground and speak her name softly into the darkness.

"Dìomath?"

The silken silence feels like ruin.

I move deeper into the underground cavity, feeling along the packed wall, my eyes struggling to adjust to the murk. The sweet-earth smell is reassuring, reminiscent of my enchantress, but all the breath leaves me when I see her—

She lies on the ground, spring-bright eyes hidden under their lids, once-perked lips and cheeks slack with sleep. Curled in on herself, tucked beneath a low slope of the cave's ceiling in a nest of brush and never-fall needles, she looks as if she prepared for this rest.

Did she know such sleep was coming?

I shake my head in horror as I regard Dìomath, the full-ness of her bear form the only thing in my sight. I touch the fur behind her ear, wondering if she knew. Would sleep have come upon her even if she remained human during the time I played Ràithne? Surely she wouldn't have *chosen* this form if the other would have left her unaffected by spring's change.

Perhaps her bear goddess blood was too strong, and she would have succumbed either way—perhaps this was the more comfortable choice.

I look upon my enchantress, beautiful even as a beast, the image of her uncorrupted and preserved as ever.

And I wonder—

Were we a doomed affair from the start?

A flame has scorched through me. My chest feels like the black hollow left from a fire, and my eyes burn as I stare into a steaming bowl of amber tea. I can't recall having blinked since I trudged back from Bairnhart—from where I left Dìomath in hibernation.

It was an impossibility, but I feel stupid for having failed to consider it.

Nathaire listens as I sob, then leaves me with my tea, though I don't feel like imbibing.

I don't feel like much at all.

Hope is a horrible, blinding thing.

My hair begins to drive me mad as I work supple branches into the gaps of the goat enclosure, where a bear tore through and gutted most of the herd.

It has been half a day since I found my enchantress surrendered to the lull of spring's passing, but it feels like an eternity. I had dreamt of her here, with me, free of the forest and shining under the uninhibited rays of the summer sun. I had imagined her beaming as Onora colored her face with brightness, and her twinkling laugh as Nathaire taught her his silent language. I had fantasized of her persuading me from my morning hunt to draw me back to her warmth, the golden virtue of her whisper granting my every wish.

But she is not here, and so I've busied myself with labor.

It's familiar work, which is why I've taken it upon myself, but noticeably absent is the waxy prickle of bearsbane that I long ago made a habit of weaving into the plaits.

It's ration that urges me to forgo the extra warding—the bearsbane has no use without bears, besides mild soothing of burns—but it's something else that urges me to keep the garlands nearby.

No bears, no bearsbane, no Dìomath.

Acceptance is a fickle, stubborn thing.

And my hair is driving me mad.

Though I knot it at the back of my head, strands fall into my face and get tangled in the wattle fencing as I work. My scalp prickles painfully from the weight and the heat and the pulling, and I do not feel like a warrior.

I shouldn't care how I'm perceived any longer—I'm hardly Bearslayer anymore, after all—but it's my own perception that dawdles.

What do I want to be if not a warrior, a mother, or a descendant of the Dagda?

"And what has your hair to do with any of that, anyway?" I mutter, snapping a bramble of auburn curls free from where they snagged in the fence.

"What of your hair?" a faltering voice asks.

I turn to see Onora stopped on the path to the well, her skirts pulled up into a makeshift basket teeming with stained bandages and cloths.

Straightening quickly, I grasp for words. "Onora—I—my hair. It's a state, isn't it?"

"Always has been." The words are clipped and cold. She doesn't meet my eyes.

"I-I'm thinking of cutting it off. To the bees with it."

She shifts her skirts, and a bandage tumbles to the ground, a red smear of warning opening to the sky. "Perhaps you should."

I move to retrieve the bandage but she snatches it up, ducks a nod, and hurries down the path and away.

Tears sting my eyes as I watch her go, but resolve hardens in my core.

Spring was an ending.

This flailing, this uncertainty—it, too, needs an ending.

I unsheathe Thornfury, and under the lazy-eyed and disapproving glare of Hazelfeur's surviving goats, I bring the blade to my chin.

I t was not quite as simple of a feat as I thought it would be, and halfway through my arms burn from the work.

Hacking off my mane is more work than slaying bears—but it is a beginning.

When I am finished, I leave the long lengths of hair scattered for the crows. I bend to pick up the strings of bearsbane lying at my feet—my curls are too short to torment my sight; the ends merely tickle my ears—and I resolutely work them into the freshly-patched fence.

The fire that had blazed me through reignites, and I hurry to my hut, keeping away from the slow-moving villagers who clog Hazelfeur's pathways like a drought. Even had I spat in their faces, I don't think they would have acknowledged me.

Has it always been this way?

Nathaire has vacated my roundhouse, and I find it odd that the badger is gone with him—its skin is gone, too, and not drying near the hearth—but if he were here, he would know what I intended to do, so it is good that he has left.

I take Ràithne upon my back and slip outside before I

can give it further thought.

Making my way around the outskirts of the village, I catch sight of Maira, the girl who lost her beloved at springtide. She's coming away from the hawthorn tree, and seeing her jars me, giving me pause—long enough pause for her to notice me creeping toward Bairnhart with a harp upon my shoulders.

Her expression, at first, is shrouded in shadow, the hollows of her cheeks pronounced by insatiable hunger for the reality she once knew. Then, coming nearer, her lips twist and the shadows recede almost forcefully.

"Rhoswen," she says brightly, standing on her toes to kiss my cheek. The kindness in her voice is shorn through with sadness, but nothing akin to the blame I expected. Her gaze lingers on my hair for a breath. "The púca said it was you who turned the tides of spring. I was—" She swallows and flushes. "Ah...they frighten me. I was told never to believe them, but of course it was you. You've always been so brave."

I fishmouth stupidly, shifting Ràithne on my back. "I-I'm unsure if it's a...permanent solution. Without spring—"

"You deserve thanks, Rhoswen," Maira insists. Her eyebrows pinch. "The elders were slow to make change. It shouldn't have fallen on you..." She laughs, and though the sound is full, it sounds as if someone whacked it out of her. "Áine knows I *never* would have picked up a blade."

"You're kind," I murmur, though I feel worse for her praise.

"I have hope that we can hold a feast in your honor. I know there's much to be done—my family's home was cleaved in two—but perhaps it's what we need." She smiles and then nods her leave.

When she is several paces away she looks back, wringing her hands, gaunt-faced again and forehead wrinkled. The absent smile fades as her eyes flit to Ràithne. Then she continues on.

"Godsdamn you, Maira," I say under my breath, but still make haste for the forest.

My passage into Bairnhart is interrupted just beyond the treeline. Jumpy as a piskie trapped in a child's fingers, I freeze in my tracks at a strange rustling, nearly dropping Ràithne in favor of Thornfury until the bumbling flat-backed critter waddles into view.

It's only a badger.

It appears to be merely hurt, at first; it walks with a jolting limp, joints popping drily.

Then I notice the way the fur sluices off of the creature, its hide grotesquely loose, grey meat and mealy gristle gaping through torn flesh.

It's a bloody wraith.

I scream, more disconcerted by the undead badger than I would be by an army of wraithbears. Ràithne slides free of my grip, thumping to the ground, and Thornfury glides eagerly into my palm. I draw my wrist back to crack his chain.

A hand clamps down on my wrist. Nathaire is suddenly there, shoving me backward, and the badger scuttles off into the brush.

"What—Nathaire—what in the Dagda's fresh—"

"*Roz, it was me,*" his hands sign frantically. He looks sheepish, as if I've just caught him staring at a goat's backside for two seconds too long.

"Nathaire—a wraith—a wraith*badger*—"

He reaches into the neck of his tunic, pulling something from beneath—the pendant I wondered at earlier. Without saying anything, he slips the cord off his neck and offers it to me.

Still seeing red, I take a cursory look at the object in my grip. "A...horn?"

He nods. "*Cernunnos's horn. I found it in Hazelfeur. It called to me.*"

His words take a moment to find root, but they prickle with familiarity. I frown and inspect the horn more closely. It's a simple construct of polished bone, with a bronze mouth made to look like the upturned, open-mouthed snout of a boar.

An enchantment over the earth, such that the horn could not be raised but by the strum of his harp by his daughter's hand...

"The Dagda spoke of this," I say with certainty, turning it over in my hands. The streaks of dirt clotting the ivory speak of a recent excavation. "This is...dangerous. Unnatural. It was buried for a reason."

Nathaire shakes his head. "*It is a thing of power. That does not make it dangerous.*"

Depends on its wielder, I nearly say, but I bite my tongue, remembering for what reason I brought a similar such thing

266

of power to this forest.

"Be careful, Natty," I say, and return the horn to his steady hand.

He casts a look at Ràithne behind me, and his face darkens. He moves as if to hinder me from venturing further, and his eyebrows tick upward, one of them nearly snug to his hairline.

"It's not what you think," I spout, though it is likely exactly what he thinks.

"*You are a dreadful liar.*"

"I am not!"

"*Your face is red as a wee one's slapped rear.*"

I wrinkle my nose, seizing the digression and mentally cursing the quickness of my blood's rising. "You've seen a wee one's slapped rear?"

He doesn't blink, and I cow beneath his gaze.

"I-I have to wake her, Nathaire. She wants so badly to be free, and *I* want her so badly to be free, and just because she has bear blood..." I trail off, squeezing my fingertips. "Just let me wake her, if even for a moment. I want her to know I won't stop—"

"*You would endanger our people for her.*" His irises spark, molten gold inflaming and annealing.

"Our people do not *care* what I do." I intend my voice to be sharp, but it is whip-thin and reedy. "Nor have they ever. Today marks the first day I have received gratitudes from *any* of them. Not even Onora has offered me thanks before, only patched me up and sent me on my way. I—I can't *do* it any longer, Nathaire, I only swore myself Bearslayer so I wouldn't be cast from the village, but even that....even that wasn't enough to become well and truly a part of it. You can't tell me you haven't felt the same."

Nathaire's knuckles whiten around his horn. "*Things will be different now.*"

"For you, perhaps," I murmur, "but I must find purpose elsewhere."

"*Where?*" he asks, his finger a warped spear bespeaking the woods surrounding us. "*Here?*"

"If she'll have me," I say.

"*And what of Artio?*"

I swallow the lump in my throat. "If she has issue with me, she'll speak it. I will...I don't know. I will parley with her on Hazelfeur's behalf. Isn't that enough? Can't I be done with this duty?"

"*That is not up to me.*" He thumbs a rogue tear from my cheek, smiling sadly, then flicks at a chunk of hair hanging from my crown. "*I wondered when you would be rid of that mess on your head.*"

"It's alright, isn't it?" I ask, patting at the shorn patches of scalp extending from my temple. "I feel a bit like that impish bard whose eye you nearly took out at solstice— remember, with the silver hair?"

He contemplates me. "*If you had a smaller nose, perhaps, and bigger breasts.*"

"Natty!" I swat his wrist. "We cannot all be as shapely as you, god of goatheads. And I am not so chivalrous as to be above making crude jests at your granddaughter's expense. What say you?"

He snorts and shakes his head vigorously. *"I beg mercy."*

I touch Ràithne's wood; hesitant, hopeful. "Please, Nathaire."

"Only because you are so wretchedly moon-eyed," he signs, wiggling his fingers. Then he lifts the harp as if it's a child and follows me into the forest.

hough free of snow-weight, the trees and fauna of the underbrush bow toward us as we stand in the clearing. They hunch like quickly aging men, and with the same reverence, the same ambivalence for that which cannot be understood—time, life, love, spirit.

They bow to us, and no one knows why but for the assumed notion that when there is nothing else, there is the divine.

I think we have it wrong, though.

It is the trees and the mountains and the clouds, after all, who cast us in shadow.

athaire chooses to remain above ground, and while I sense his unease, I strangely don't share it. As I lower myself into Dìomath's hollow, my heartbeat quickens, but only in anticipation, not fear. I even search for the anxiety, certain it must be there after all I endured to change the seasons, but undoing my work seems preordained.

Waking my enchantress is marked out in the stars. It is the only destiny I know.

Nathaire stoops at the mouth of the hollow, peering into the darkness. *"This is where your lover rests?"*

"Aye," I say, breathless and bouncing on my toes, keen to commune with Ràithne and wake Dìomath.

Nathaire passes the harp down to me. *"You may not have long. The bears have not slept more than a day, so they will wake easily."*

Holding Raithne to my chest, I busy myself with her placement in the musty-sweet den and pray he believes haste is the cause for the heat in my cheeks.

"Take the time you need," he signs, pressing closer to the edge of the hole. If he hopes to look me in the eye, I pretend

not to notice. "*No longer.*"

"No longer," I agree, and that, at least, is not a lie—for how could he understand how much time I need when it comes to her?

As my hands hover, poised abreast of Ràithne's strings, I feel a sudden rush of excitement, so different from the dread I've come to know at spring's awakening.

I could come to love an eternal spring, I think.

I would, for her.

I don't rush Ràithne's song. She tells me magic can't be made with haste, and so I set forth the intricacies of my wishes, and we take our time. The sound is like infinitesimal droplets humming along a spider's web, capturing winks of light just to leave them behind upon the threads, spilling refracted illusions onto the earth. Delicate, timeless.

At the song's tapering, as the earth struggles to comprehend the divergence of the light-noise, spreading the rays farther and wider until they are but fingers of the tiniest gossamer creature, Dìomath begins to rouse.

Her rich chestnut fur ripples, shoulder blades steepling with quickening breath. Her paws flex and elegant, unstained claws flash white then retract, curling fetally into cowlicked tufts. Her ears twitch and tuck forward as if dancing.

As my fingers lift from Ràithne's strings, Dìomath's eyelids spring apart.

"Enchantress," I whisper, and the face of what I once thought of as my enemy regards me with a warmth I've never known.

She lifts herself up, and in a blink she's standing before me, smaller and unfurred, the eyes and nose and mouth I know so well shaping first a smile—*My rose*—a concern—*You woke me!*—a question—*What's happened?* —and then a laugh as I shatter myself upon her lips.

When I am finished kissing her thoroughly, she asks me again, "What's happened? Why did you wake me?"

"Because I am lost to you," I surrender, and kiss her further. Then I gesture to Ràithne. "You told me to play her, Dìomath. Why didn't you tell me it would cause you to sleep with the rest of Artio's children?"

She slips her hand around the back of my neck, and I shiver as her fingers tickle my nape. "It had to be done. But it brought you back to me. I knew it would."

Her words strike me as strange, but my mind's clarity dissolves under her touch and I don't care, I don't care, I don't care.

"You brought someone," she says, chin pointed toward the light from above. With a curious smile, she slips her hand into mine. "Let's join them."

Gods and crows above, I think, her voice an ambrosia drawing me to the surface.

I would follow her anywhere.

I scramble up the wall of the hollow, hauling Ràithne behind me, and then help Dìomath, thrilling at her giggle when she slips on the edge and tumbles into my arms.

Several paces away, Nathaire looks over his shoulder

from where he stands in the clearing, an arrow nocked in his bow and daggered toward the trees beyond. He glances at me first, then at my enchantress brushing off her skirts. I hardly see him move, but with the quickness of a breeze he swivels on his heel, arms locked in their drawn position, and suddenly the jagged flint tip of his arrow is leveled at Dìomath's heart.

My gut seizes viciously as I move in front of her, my breath withering in my lungs. I stand there for a moment, staring hard at Nathaire, confused and horrified.

He only glares over my shoulder at Dìomath, and with his hands tight on his bow he says nothing.

"*Nathaire,*" I gasp, spreading my fingers outward—placating, begging. What is it he always tells me? I press strength into my voice. "*Calm.* This is Dìomath, Natty."

He takes one hand off his bow, pinning the arrow in its place with the other on the grip as he stabs a finger at her and then thumbs his chin—"*She is not.*"

My temples ache with the depth of my frown. "Lower your aim," I command shakily.

He does not move.

"Nathaire, please..." Would I wield Thornfury against him, if it came to protecting her? "If this is about spring, we'll find another way—"

"*It is not,*" he signs, then again jabs a finger over my shoulder. "*She is not.*"

"I don't understand. Would you please—"

The bow finally falls from his grip. His hands slash

through the air, his gestures nearly as fierce as the razor-sharp lines of his face, and his body jolts with each move-ment.

"*She. Is. Not. Diomath.*"

My ears ring. My palms run slick. I don't dare speak.

"*She. Is. Artio.*"

Nathaire has never lied to me—except perhaps to reassure me I didn't look a sight after a scrape with a particularly rotten wraithbear and my ensuing struggle to respire without tears—and yet, in this moment—this truly unforeseen, unsought moment—I doubt him.

I want to tell him he's wrong, that his suspicions are mere fodder for the bees and my silly anxieties have rubbed off on him.

I want to tell him his being a god hardly means he knows all, that gods have gotten it wrong before and that sometimes feelings must be ignored.

I want to tell him to sod off and let me have this little happiness, this great love, this slice of divinity.

I doubt him, because it terrifies me to think of what a fool I've been.

𝕴 don't know how long I stand there, silent and unmoving, the bloodrush in my ears a terrible, roaring maelstrom I wish would sweep me up bodily and deposit me far from here, somewhere cold and free of gods.

It's not until I hear them approach, awake and attuned to their mother, that I press my hand to my hip. Thornfury feels like a weighted block of ice; I've never wanted to brandish him less than I do in this moment.

I turn around to face Dìomath, now flanked quietly by bearspawn emerging from the woods, a singular beauty among the peaked faces. She looks no different than before.

"I-I don't understand." The words come out a croak, and it is that by which I am humiliated most.

Dìomath holds out a steadying hand and tilts her head to the side, exposing a soft stretch of neck. "I will explain all, I promise you. Do you trust me, my rose?"

my rose

my rose

my rose

I have forgotten how to breathe.

I think Thornfury falls from my hand.

I care not if Nathaire still points an arrow at my spine.

Did I know it was her?

Did I know all along?

"Rhoswen," Dìomath murmurs, and I am but a speck trapped in amber. "I will explain everything, the truth of it all, but your father is here, and he means me harm."

I frown. "My...father...?"

And Bairnhart Forest erupts in a madness of gods.

*I*t has always been me against the bears.

They are simple enemies, if not in their nature as beasts then in their nature as it pertains to my world—namely, that I share no bond with them. Our relationship is one of attack and defense and it is easy to understand, nothing existing between us but the intrinsic fight to survive. On my part, necessity prevails above all: the bears harm my people, and they meet their death at my hand.

But it is not just the bears now.

As a very large, very familiar she-boar bursts into the clearing, snorting a frenzy and hoofs wildly clouting the bearspawn clawing her from all sides, I wonder if the complexity of the situation has manifested as clearly to Nathaire as it has to me. Now that the Dagda is here, we're both suddenly in the presence of kin we've only just discovered— my father and his daughter, though I've yet to come to terms with the implications of either.

So, too, have I realized the relationships between the rest of them precede my life entirely, and there is much I don't—and don't wish to—understand.

And yet the *only* thing I can see clearly as the three gods clash among the trees...is her.

Dìomath. Artio.

Enchantress. Deceitress.

By the time I shake myself free of my trance, the Dagda has leapt from Gobby's saddle, leaving the boar to fend for herself against a swarm of wraithbears as he rages across the clearing, a massive club raised above his head. His cold blue eyes are trained on Dìomath, but as Nathaire draws an arrow he whirls, blocking his body with the club. Recognition dawns white upon his face and he barks out what I realize is—*was*—Nathaire's name.

"Cernunnos."

Nathaire might as well be a statue for the steadiness of his hand, and I wonder how much he remembers of his most recent death. I cannot tell if it is indifference or vengeance in his gaze.

The Dagda pitches a mirthless laugh, looking between Nathaire and Dìomath as if one is a hunter and the other is prey. "Have you discovered it was she who plotted your demise? Is that why you're here, o horned one, to rain retribution on your wicked daughter?"

She is not wicked, I think, but I don't wish to break the tension for fear that Nathaire's arrow may yet fly.

Nathaire shifts his weight, betraying his uncertainty, but it is Dìomath who speaks next.

"I was not *wicked* until you made me so," she spits, and the pain in her voice cleaves me in two. "And my father

284

knew I would seek my freedom. He just didn't know by whose hand it would come."

"You will never be freed from this place, not after what you've done." The Dagda watches Nathaire for a moment and then, seeming assured of his old enemy's inaction, wheels on Dìomath. He stops short when a bear I am certain is Éamon rears at him. "You took *everythin'* from me, you deceitful creature, and you dare antagonize me?"

"I did not take everything," Dìomath says simply, and her eyes find mine. Her voice is a serenity. "You only failed to see what I left behind."

The Dagda follows her gaze, and I find myself netted beneath their piercing stares. With Thornfury on the ground and nothing to occupy my hands, I fumble awkwardly and step back, bumping into Ràithne.

It is then the Dagda seems to absorb a number of things very quickly, his face contorting with each one.

I worry he will blame me for the deaths of his sons. I know I deserve it—I know it's the truth. The brothers died because of me. And I stole his harp as they breathed their last.

But what fills the Dagda's face, at the end of its contorting, is not anger. "You played Ràithne," he says, a strange intensity warbling his voice.

I swallow hard and nod. "Aye. I did. I played her right well, if you ask me."

Dìomath slips her hand into mine, igniting me with breath, and I let my grasp tether me to her—to my enchantress—deciding to decipher all other feelings concerning her identity later.

"Rhoswen is the daughter you bore with your mortal lover," she declares, and the Dagda seems to crumple in on himself. "You killed my father, as I begged you to, but it did nothing to free me. If anything, you only trapped me deeper in despair with your disloyalty."

"What....vile...animal," the Dagda hisses, words honed into spears, "takes a child from the womb of its dead mother?"

Dìomath's hand spasms in mine. She seems to wait for me to pull away, but I don't, and so she carries on. "The kind to whom you pledged your heart."

"Jealous, spiteful *witch!* Y'only loved me because I had the means to free you. You would've loved any beast who found you in your sorry state. Isn't that what this is?" He gestures to our clasped hands.

"You know nothing of what this is."

There's a pause, pregnant with suspense. Both of them silent, both seething.

Then, "I think you should leave."

The words lilt from my lips too lightly for the matter at hand. I level my stare boldly with the Dagda's.

"I will not bear witness to what you came here to do," I tell him. If my voice shakes, I hope Dìomath doesn't hear it. "You refused to help me, and I did without your aid. None of this is yours to bear any longer. These woods aren't yours, nor is Hazelfeur. If Nathaire wishes to settle honor with you, it is not of my concern, but you...you're a god best forgotten."

The Dagda barely acknowledges my words, only sneers. "You're a fool, daughter," he says, and raises his club.

It is a very different thing, to fight for a person rather than a people.

The Dagda's club arcs down toward Dìomath and, despite my shock—despite everything—I surge into action with the fury of a thousand suns. I seize Ràithne, silently offering her an apology for it, and swing the harp to block the Dagda's blow. Wood cracks on wood, but they must be molded from the same enchanted oak because neither takes so much as a splinter from the other.

The Dagda hefts his club, raking me with a look of utter scorn. He is oblivious to or else uncaring of Nathaire's drawn arrow following his every move. "You do not know what you protect, child," he raves, the dampness in his tone gone. "Cease this nonsense!"

I hook my toe under Thornfury's chain, drag it nearer, and pluck him up from the ground. My scars blaze with itch as I tell the Dagda, "I have no misgivings about doing battle with you."

His nostrils flare. "Nor do I."

"*No,*" Dìomath breathes from behind me. At her inflection, Éamon rears again, but she silences him with a fist. "Do this one thing right, and let—"

"I will never do a thing more for you," the Dagda spits.

"Not for me, you buffoon," she retorts, and I nearly laugh, so strange it is to hear such a word from her delicate lips. "For her. For your blood. She is more than you will ever be—more than either of us could aspire towards. Is she not?"

Nothing dawns on the Dagda's face. His gaze is unaffected, his eyes forever limned by a dark insensibility.

"If you have no affection for me," I say, my voice raw, "then think of my mother."

A breath.

"The roses on your mountain...were they not for her? The only thing you cared for. I noticed that."

The loose skin of his throat quivers, and his club drops an inch. His glare flickers, but hardens again when he glances over my shoulder. "I'll not speak o' her here."

"Is it too much to ask her name?"

"It is," he says, but his expression spools with emotion. The rage thins, fracturing beneath the weight of memory. "Anwena."

My breath catches. *Anwena.*

A mother's name.

My mother's name.

"She was...a thing to behold." The Dagda lowers his club fully. "Not just in sight, but in ev'ry sense."

I notice a change in the air, a sharpening, but the Dagda

is lost to remembering a love long dead.

"The roses were her soul, the wind her song. A woman like that...nothin' like it. Nothin' will ever come close."

His next words are cut off by Éamon's roar and the thunderous rush of fleshbears plowing into the clearing, a deluge of them descending upon the Dagda and Gobby, who bellows at her master's plight and charges from within a mass of untiring wraithbears.

Instinct hums through my veins, but before flinging Thornfury into the fray I catch sight of Dìomath standing rigid, wrath riddled into the furrow of her brow and the press of her lips. Where she had been holding aloft a fist to keep Éamon and his brethren at bay, now her fingers are splayed, clemency tossed to the breeze.

"Dìo—" My plea to her is cut off by the whistle of an arrow past my ear. Emerald feathers streak just shy of Dìomath's cheekbone and Nathaire's arrow lands solidly in the alder tree beyond her.

Incensed by the opportunity to bewreak his attempt on her life, Dìomath morphs before my eyes, every feature elongating and every pore bristling until she stands double my height and blanketed in fur.

In this form, all the power and indignation of nature radiates from her, its prowess hers to command.

She falls upon Nathaire, and even as I scream I am in awe of her.

Always a thing to behold, even in savagery.

Ìomath sweeps her claws across Nathaire's chest, and Nathaire draws a curved blade from his hip to level her with equally sharp strikes at her breast. The Dagda holds his own against Dìomath's bears, club swinging wildly, and the bears aggress with little restraint.

The air grows thick with blood and hubris, and though I am at the heart of this story, this clash between gods, I do not feel a part of it.

I feel as if I am again dreaming, watching from some immaterial plane, unable to separate the pieces from the whole, though I see both; though I see all.

Bad blood runs between these gods, these three beings who I pretend to understand. But as I watch them, I come to notice something, perhaps a most important thing.

In this moment, they are not gods.

They maintain the pride of Cernunnos and Artio and the Dagda. Centuries of hate and love and pain force them to move, to fight, to kill, all of it is ingrained in those names—the names they were given for their power; the names given at a time when something bigger was needed, something in which faith could be placed.

But I see it boiled down before me: hate, love, pain.

The worst things, the best things.

Human things.

And humans, unlike bears, can always see reason.

Or so I hope.

I lay Thornfury down beside Ràithne, and I can't help but squeeze my fingertips as I step into the fray.

Onetwothree, onetwothree, onetwothree.

I approach the Dagda first. The bears packed around him part a little—whether by their own volition or Dìomath's sway I cannot tell—and it's enough for me to squeeze through and show my face.

The Dagda brings his club down with the cry of a warrior who has tired of his duty, crushing a bear's skull before his bearded chin whips around and he locks eyes with me.

"Leave," I tell him as his club swings up into a wraith-bear's maggoted ribcage. "Grieve your sons, and do it properly, without spirits in your belly. Give them the love they deserved in life. Find your dignity—Finín told me you kept it around somewhere, said you were a better man than you were a god. And that's not for you to take offense at, it's the truth. We'd all do well to focus on ourselves rather than notions of godliness."

Still fending off Éamon and his ilk, the Dagda gapes at me between swings, and as I speak I can't tell if any part of him heeds my words. Then he casts a venomous glance in Dìomath's direction, so I take a breath and press on.

"I admit I've had whims of family, but I'm *not* a fool. I know what it is to not want children, and I know tenderness is lost with the years. You needn't be my father, but, by the crows, you are *a* father, even in their death." I step forward, and when the bears fall back I do not believe it to be Dìomath's command. "You've borne so much pain, and that is something I know of, too. Find your strength. Find your heart."

The fierceness seems to trickle out of him. He pants heavily, appraising the hovering bearspawn, but his club falls to his side. "Daughter—Rhoswen—"

"Find *yourself*, old man," I snap, boldened by the way my name burdens his tongue. "And find that leprechaun fecker and get your sons their clothes back, too."

Without waiting for a response, I turn away from the once-god and move on to the next.

Onetwothree, onetwothree.

Dìomath and Nathaire are locked in battle, both bloodied and with fire in their eyes.

"I just ordered the Dagda away," I say, more uncomfortable with them for the intimacies we've shared.

By some strong sweep of luck it garners their attention. Their mutual enmity toward the Dagda breaks them apart, and Dìomath roars as the Dagda hoists himself onto Gobby's back. She makes to go after him, but I capture one of her paws between my hands and press the soft pads to my cheek, ignoring the scrape of her claws in my hair.

"Please let him go," I urge her, knowing that were she to

ignore my asking I would be unable to stop her. "He has caused you suffering, yes, but so too were *you* the cause of *his*. Please, Dìomath. Come back to me."

Dìomath turns away from the receding boar and its rider, but there is still a blaze in her eyes—one I distantly recognize as inextinguishable, and yet still I press myself close to her.

"Please," I say again, praying the threads of enchantment that bind us are strong enough to sway the blaze.

But for Artio, the moment is one under her vengeful domain. She tears her paw from my grasp, hurtling past me to crush Nathaire to the ground, and then just as quickly pelts away from him and disappears into the forest.

My vision blurs as I watch her go, and red edges in as I rush to Nathaire's side. He's sprawled on the ground, wheezing and clutching his chest.

"Natty," I gasp, pressing my hands along his torso to feel for injuries. "Where—"

He rolls to his side and slaps away my clumsy fingers with a wince, palming his chest. He looks up at me, horn buds poking through his hair, and signs urgently, *"She took the horn."*

But the words do little to pierce my concern for the blood on his tunic, and I try to shove him onto his back. "Where is the blood coming from? Can you breathe? Stop trying to sit, Natty—"

"No," he signs, and after a moment of swatting uselessly at each other he manages to capture my wrists. With his

other hand he reaches for the cord around his neck, and when he pulls it from beneath his tunic, there's nothing at the end of it.

And I realize what it was in Artio's eyes that rendered her unreasonable.

It was the look of a mother hoping to bring her children back from death.

As I race through the forest after the She-Bear, so too does my mind race with thoughts of her deception, and every thought churns my insides and slicks my throat with bile.

The thoughts stretch back eleven equinoxes, back to when I had thought it the crows' whimsy that I happened upon Artio's lair. I had fallen into the den of bears and swung wildly at the waking beasts with my unchristened scythe, and that springtide voice had told me to wait.

It is not time yet, my rose.

not time yet

not time yet

not time yet

I think I understand, now, why they hid her in the forest.
She had been my only thought. My only dream.
And she had not been true.

know what Artio intends to do with Cernunnos's horn of renascence—free herself from Bairnhart, and free her dead children from the snares of Morrigan's blackened talons. All the bears Nathaire and I have put to rest—eleven equinoxes' worth—will be raised from their graves. And Artio will be free to rule over them without bound.

Even knowing Hazelfeur hosts a mass grave of bear-spawn, I hesitate when I find her at the edge of the forest, a maiden once again, and I even hesitate when she raises the bronze-and-bone horn to her lips.

For a breath I wonder what would happen if I allowed her to give air to the horn. I wonder if its magic would take effect instantly; if the bears would rise as wraiths from the earth and start their new life by laying ruin to their death-bed. Or would the magic ooze outward slowly, creeping first into the nearest bodies and picking through them, one by one, tirelessly working to restore what has long since decomposed?

The method hardly matters. For a breath I consider it—the chaos falling upon Hazelfeur, putting an end to my long war with the bears.

But they once called me Bearslayer, and though it is just a name, it is one I gave myself. It is one *I* have faith in, even if no one else does.

I curl my toes into the dirt and bow forward, my body coiling and then uncoiling, my elbow snapping straight and my wrist flicking out with a soft click of bone, worn leather curved tight against rough calluses, crescent-moon fingernails pressed to the grooves of my palm, all of it a prayer. And so Thornfury flies.

My blade swings true, and there's a muted, hollow echo as the horn flies from Artio's hands.

"Was it all a deceit?" I ask. It is a small triumph that my voice doesn't break.

She looks at me—Dìomath? Artio? If there is a difference, I cannot tell—and tears pearl in her eyes. With the blood on her dress, she is the girl I first encountered, the one who first enchanted me, the one who enchants me still.

You weak, weak thing.

I curse myself as I'm drawn to her; as I fall to my knees before her. She is only anguish, and, yet still, I let her suffocate me.

She touches my face, sliding silken fingertips along my jaw. "My feelings were true, but you cannot understand, Rhoswen, the love I have for my children—"

"You sought to destroy my home, manipulated me to do your bidding, *used* me to seek out the Dagda's harp and raise your father's horn—for you knew I could, you devised it as such from the moment you carved me out of my mother's womb, didn't you?" I meet her eyes, my gaze impressing upon her the fullness of my hurt, the shattering of the pedestal I beheld her on, the sheer magnitude of her betrayal. Fury steals my voice. "And yet you say the feelings were not a lie. How can that be true?"

She shakes her head, presses both hands to my face, and leans so close as to steal the breath from my mouth. "Because, now that I can be free, I can give you *so much more*."

I close my eyes, knowing she must feel the rapid *un un un* of my heart in my throat, the cursed thing laying bare my inability to despise her.

"I had—a child, Rhoswen," she whispers, so quietly I almost don't hear. "My first. Does that give it more weight, that he was my first? It certainly felt like it, at the time. He was dazzling. The brightest thing I'd ever seen."

Her voice disappears into a sob, and the noise is a void of the deepest, most tragic misery. I open my eyes, and the pinch of her face is a horrible, ungodly thing, ugly in the sense that no soul should ever feel such a way.

"Dìomath..."

"It made it all the more painful when his light began to dim. He grew sick, and I never knew if it—was it something I had done, or failed to do? Could I have... done *more?*" The tears, for all their smallness, wrack her body with a terrible trembling. "I watched him die. Death is many things, but it is not fair. I think whatever light I had in me went out with his, and I lost my grip on what life meant. No—on what *giving* life meant."

I realize I am clutching her as if to pull one of us—I am not sure which—to safety. "The horn..."

She nods. "My father used it for trivial things. He kept up weeds and brambles, things that needn't have lived, and he called it balance. I only wanted to see if I could wield it. I practiced on rabbits, but it wasn't enough, it was still too small a thing, and I didn't know how—how to breathe *enough* life into it, so that it wasn't so awful..."

"Death cannot be made into anything but awful, Dìo-math, not to those of us left living."

"No, but it can be *un*made," she says, and I feel her being pulled toward Cernunnos's horn where it landed a mere pace away. I tighten my grip on her. "I had more children before I tried again. They had natural deaths, at the end of long lives, so I could bear it to see them go. But the horn made them into horrid creatures of the night—I didn't lie, when I told you I have little love for them."

I cup my hand to the base of her skull, feeling her heart beating even faster than mine. Where the Dagda told his tale as if describing a flower, Dìomath spills hers as if re-calling a time she drowned.

"When my father found what I'd done, he banished me. His balance was be-all, and I'd decimated it. But that horn, its power..." Her voice again collapses. "*Why* couldn't it be meant to give light back to that which once shone?"

She moves suddenly, buckling beneath long-stifled sobs as she falls toward me—for a closer embrace, I think, and curl my shoulders to shelter her—but then I hear the rustle of leafmould, fingers upon something hollow, and just as suddenly she's springing away from me.

And then she is bringing Cernunnos's carnyx to her mouth, and from it comes the sound of death.

In the breath following the horn's harsh blare, I comprehend the terrible, beautiful power of memory—perhaps more powerful than hope, for all its ability to befog even the minds of gods.

I see Dìomath and Artio both as she wrings the bone horn between alabaster fingers, a past and a present and nothing in between but an ashen cloud of grief.

Artio's anger is there, in the rigid posture and the blazing eyes, but so too is Dìomath's despair in the pleat of her brow and the vise of her grip.

As the horn's echo fades and the earth rumbles faintly, Artio lifts her foot from the forest floor. With a tentative, chaste stretch of her leg, she steps across the tree line.

Free of the forest, she turns to me. Her jaw quivers.

"I am well and truly sorry for what I have done," Dìomath whispers, the dark luster lifting from her gaze and then again silvering her eyes with teeth-blunting flintiness.

She takes to her heels and flees for Hazelfeur.

ead bears begin to rise as wraiths all around me, and I am strangely grateful for them. They keep me from that sickening, slow crawl to anger and its repressive hold, that boldest of feelings the most difficult to overcome, and instead what feathers through me is an icy bolt of cowardice followed by a fiery burst of mettle.

As a pair of wraithbears approaches in a squall of rotten flesh, shedding the husks of earth they rose from, I mutter, "*Why* do my Bearslaying days *so* refuse to end?"

I find Thornfury's handle and hoist the crest of his blade aloft, but I pause before slinging his chain, searching the voids of the wraiths' eyes for any semblance of vitality.

But I only feel sorry for the ugly beasts; though they may live, without that soft glimmer of light they are not alive. There is no brink which they may climb over to be free of death, no bared membranes with which to absorb sunlight—

They cannot grow. They can have no better purpose.

I cut through the two spiritless creatures, and all the rest that quickly follow, but I know they could merely rise anew were Dìomath to blow the horn again. I edge past the treeline, desperate to fight through to Hazelfeur, but the wraiths swarm thicker and stronger. I realize this is where most of the fleshbears once fell at my hand, cut down before they could make a beeline for the village, and now it is where most of them rise from a mass grave.

Suddenly I lose my footing and tumble into the freshly disturbed rut of earth. I gasp for breath and fumble with Thornfury as the wraithbears descend, unable to find footing among the loose soil and broken spears of bone. I slash wildly at the monsters, a scream caught in my throat, the horrible stench of canker and blight stinging my eyes. Black rot sprays my face, blinding me so I can't tell one wraith from the next, and I must be partway down one's gaping throat when a firm hand grasps my arm and yanks me from the ichorous furor.

Nathaire's face appears through the blur. As I swipe away muck, I see his hands slant sharply over my head: "Go." Emerald iridescence stipples the ground around us, a stark contrast against the smattered pitch of sinew pinned beneath the arrows.

"GO," Nathaire signs again. He shoves me, and in the same movement nocks an arrow into his bow and lets it fly.

I nod dully, trying to catch my breath, and stagger away from the fray. I run through the tall grasses as fast as my clumsy feet allow, thoughts of Dìomath and what she must be feeling like coals under my toes.

What does she intend to do once she finds her first-born? Has she found him already? Will his lack of true life destroy her, or fuel her rage?

I cannot determine which would be worse.

The risen wraithbears are a thick fog surrounding Hazelfeur, their collective movement an awful shudder, the press of their skeletal forms a frantic, impetuous slaughter. Death is all they know.

I rip through a cluster of wraithbears, my stomach knotting at the tang of hot blood in the air. My chest is so tight I fear my lungs will burst of their own accord, and the feeling draws wetness from my eyes. I cannot say what the tears are for—*the bears, Dìomath, my people, the gods*—but it doesn't matter. They don't affect the strength of my blade.

I search for Dìomath as I fight toward the center of the village, the wraiths becoming an afterthought and Thornfury slicing wind that tastes of decay as I whip through the chaos. Some villagers have taken up threshing sickles and wield them shakily, women and men sobbing alike in desperate attempts to protect children swathed in bearsbane behind them.

"The temple!" I urge, bearing quick aid before hastening them toward the unexpected safety of the púca's house, hoping that the godsforsaken sprites have taken up arms in Nathaire's old name.

The knots of dread in my stomach constrict when I see the wraiths encroaching upon Onora's hut, then strangle me to the hilt when I hear the shrill screams from within.

I wore wraith bones in my hair not for their effect on others, but to cultivate a warrior's readiness—I needed that inescapable reminder to *fear*; the toneless clack of them against each other ensured my muscles were always tense, prepared.

As I surge toward Onora's hut, terror slicks my veins with ice, and without the bones rattling near my ear I realize how silly it was to think I could train my fear. It was a thought seeded before I had a family, before I knew of love, before I realized the true effect such grim habits would have on my mind.

Thornfury's steel carves through the charred air like a falling moon, felling a wraithbear at the opening of Onora's roundhouse and clearing a path inside the hut. Cowering against the far wall—brandishing the pretty paint on her arms like armor and sprigs of bearsbane in her fists like dag-gers—is Katelia, the oldest girl.

Her screams grow threadier as a wraithbear convulses nearer, and the whites of her eyes glint like a hare at the howl of a coyote. Though she faces the wraith with arms bared, she thrusts her shoulder sidelong into the wall with an impressive show of strength. While the daub crumbles to the ground, the laths are unforgiving under her spindly frame.

I don't dare swing Thornfury in such close proximity to Katelia, so I lunge forward and plunge his scythe upward into the gristle of the wraith's grotesquely thrawn spine, so deep that my shoulder pops when I attempt to pull it free again. The wraithbear whirls before I can adjust my grip on the scythe and I lose hold of the handle altogether.

Brought horrifically close to the rancid stretch of its maw and cursing as its scraping shriek smatters me with oil-thick ichor, I plunge my hand into the maggotted cowl of meat and through the splintered sponge of its collarbone. Jagged teeth gnash against my shoulder, but I set my jaw and reach and reach and *reach*—until finally I find the scythe's handle and wrench it free, screaming needlessly as I drag it through the fiend's spine and neck.

The wraithbear collapses to the ground in a pool of black gore and dusky bones.

I hear Katelia sob and find myself similarly mewling, both of us relieved and horrified and overwhelmed. I go to her and hold her, smearing her arms with ichor.

"Alright?" I ask, and she hiccups, tiny teeth chattering. I nod, stepping back, then without hesitation press Thornfury into her pink palm. "You take this. You'll get on with him well, I think. He doesn't belong to a Bearslayer any longer... What shall you be, then? The Herbcutter of Hazelfeur?"

Her shivering eases as she inspects Thornfury, her grip on the leather strong and certain. In her fair hair, dried petals whisper softly. She can be anything she wants.

When I threaded wraith bones into my hair, it was by design that the noise would grate on my nerves, but now I wonder if I need a reminder to soothe my nerves instead.

As I guide Katelia from the hut, I wonder if Onora will gild pressed wildflowers with brightness for me to wear in the bones' stead: a reminder to breathe, to grow, to be un-afraid.

$\mathcal{I}$ don't intend to linger at the púca's temple—I only want to ensure Katelia hurries safely inside before I return to my sweep of the village. But then I hear a pleading voice deeper in the hazel grove behind the temple and, though it is coarse with despair, I know it to be Dìomath's.

I hasten into the grove, ducking under the low-hanging catkins until I see her kneeling before a patch of turned soil.

"Mathúin," she moans again and again. "Please, my Mathúin, my light..."

Her body shakes as she murmurs her pleas, and it's not until one of the hazel trees shivers and light puzzles through to where Dìomath kneels that I see what she clutches in her lap.

It writhes and snarls, a wisp of a thing long decayed, the mass of needle-thin bones a grim semblance of what it once was.

Mathúin—*bear child.*

It fights Dìomath not to hurt her but to escape, and I know it is driven toward the darkness like its brethren, destruction the only thing it knows.

Yet still Dìomath hopes it is the child she once knew, the child it can never be again.

I venture a step forward and offer her name like a prayer, and upon seeing me she grips the wraithbear tightly, cradling it to her chest even as the flinders of its fingers rake welts across her breast.

"Rhos—Rhoswen," she cries. Her eyes are red and leeched of hope, and they implore I allow her this moment.

But I shake my head. "Look at him, Dìomath. He isn't your child."

"He cannot be gone, my Mathúin—he cannot be gone from this earth." Her eyelids pinch shut, and she rocks the wraithbear frantically.

"I am so, so sorry, Dìomath," I say gently, and lower myself beside her. "He is gone from this earth, and no manipulation of time or death can change that. But he is still with you, is he not? He is still a light in your memory, and he will stay there for eternity."

Still she rocks back and forth, on the precipice of madness.

I cannot lose her.

"Look at him," I beg her. "Dìomath, please. Tell me what you see."

After a moment she obliges, and she looks upon the bundle in her arms. Tears run rivers down her face and her hair trembles as she shakes her head.

"There is no light," she whispers, and the brokenness of her voice is a scar I will wear forever.

She releases the skeletal thing but does not watch as it shudders and spasms on the ground, the deep perversion of death rendering it unable to lay waste to the living—or even to walk.

I clasp my hands to Dìomath's waist, and my knuckles brush Cernunnos's horn hidden in the fabric of her skirts. I draw it out and long to blow it, to return the wraiths to their deathbed and end it all, but I know it is not my choice to make, and instead I lay it across her thighs.

She looks at the horn, nearly folding in on herself with the silent force of her sobs. Her tongue contorts in her mouth as she considers it. Her bone-white fingers tremble as she lifts it.

Then she gives her air to the horn.

The rasp of wraith bones is punctuated by a final, sonorous clatter, and her children's suffering ceases.

Dìomath casts the horn away, and I gather her into my arms as she cries.

"I cannot know what it is to be a mother," I say softly, my lips to her temple, "nor what vivid shades of emotion must come with being one—but I do know that it is good you are feeling."

When her tears dry to salt and her shaking ceases, Dìomath untucks herself from beneath my chin, the heaven-spun green of her eyes brighter for the redness around them. The malignant manifestation of pain left untouched that had tempted her to Cernunnos's horn earlier this day seems to have dissipated with her tears.

"Do you despise me, Rhoswen?" she asks.

I frown, trailing a finger down the curve from her neck to her shoulder. "Why would I despise you?"

"Most men would. Your father does."

"Most men are fools," I murmur, dipping my thumb into the hollow of her collarbone. "And your light has not gone out, Dìomath. Darkness is only a season."

She presses her forehead to mine. "But death is not meant to be, is it?"

I shake my head, and at her fresh tears I kiss her nose, her chin, the corner of her lips. "It was wrong of your father to banish you. He left you alone at a time you needed him most. Perhaps one day he'll realize that, the old goat."

"He's young again," she concedes. "Things could be

different."

"Things can be anything we want."

"What is it you want, my rose?"

A burst of warmth greases the inside of my chest. "I-I don't—no one has ever asked me that before."

She takes her turn kissing my face. "Loneliness is only a season."

"Mm," I hum, scrunching my brow in exaggerated thought. "And hasn't the season changed?"

"It changes every day."

athaire finds us in the hazel grove as the sun drifts toward sleep. With a limp, a missing tooth, an empty quiver, and coated nearly horn to foot in wraithspawn ichor, he looks a sight. He shoots Dìomath a wary look, but the shrewd distrust in his glare eases when I offer him the boarmouthed horn.

"No more wraithbadgers," I tell him, and wait for his nod before surrendering it to him.

"No more wraiths," he amends. "Death should be left to nothingness."

We hover in heavy silence, but I sense Nathaire's discomfort at Dìomath's presence. Just as I can't fathom the feelings of mothers, nor can I fathom the feelings of gods, but I itch with the thought of his arrow pointing at her heart.

Dìomath crawls to Mathúin's bones and begins to gently return them to the upturned soil from which he rose, and I take the moment to slip away with Nathaire.

"Goldroot?" he asks, making for my hut, but I shake my head.

"You were a perfect twat in your past life, Natty," I say, because I don't know where else to begin, and he squawks in protest. "No—*listen*, you spudheaded púca-lover. You won't silence me with your dozy tea. I have much to say about men who ostracize women for their emotions, and even more to say about the same men—and those men being *you*, or leastwise *past*-you, in this matter—who keep warm a different women's bed each night.

"Now, we've decided we can be anything we want, aye? Sure, anything. But I'd advise you to not be that sort of man and, if you care for me and my woefully overzealous emotions, perhaps you'd see fit to regard Dìomath—*Dìomath*, Nathaire, not Artio—with friendliness. It can't be too difficult—you have horns, she has fur, right?"

He gawks in disbelief but blessedly keeps his hand still.

I bite my tongue, swallow hard, and the words tumble forth. "I know what she did, and I know you think me daft as Aengus's arse, but crows, Natty, I love her. And what is love, if not enduring?"

His face softens. "*It would be nothing*," he says, and drops a kiss on the top of my head.

And, though I know there is more to be said, we fall quiet with the night, reveling in that which is not nothing and hoping—as we are wont to do, gods or no—that with the love we bear, death will one day mean more than nothing, too.

AN
ENDING,
A
BEGINNING

*I*t is spring.

The world awakens from winter's languor, the passage of time untouched since the season's harbinger sang her last.

The gods have forsaken their artifacts, those illustrious trophies of old. They never belonged to the gods, after all, and were thus returned to the great trees which gave them their power.

The oaks, the alders, the willows, the hawthorns, the hazels—they no longer bow, their magic having been returned to them. They are pure and gentle rulers.

The gods have made themselves new names, ones that carry with them a sense of unimportance, of belonging, of humility. Most forget they were ever deities at all.

The one once called Artio no longer holds domain over spring, rather welcoming it as an old friend, dancing at springtide to rouse the earth into bloom and green. It is a small penitence for the upset she wrought upon the balance of life and death, but nature is forgiving.

There is no light without darkness.

She still runs among the ursine, sometimes in the shape of a maiden, lithe and wild, and other times in the shape of a bear, powerful and fierce.

She mothers the children once made into beasts, coaxing benevolence from within them, soothing the violence in their blood until they shine bright and true.

She wishes for them to be stars in the next life.

Having gained freedom from the forest which bred her grief into cruelty, she now calls the sea home. Her hair grows coarse with sea spray and her skin grows dappled with sun spots, and the one who knows her heart only loves her more for it.

The one once called Bearslayer has found her belonging.

It didn't come with the peace she expected, but peace is not what she was meant for.

She was only ever meant to grow.

Like the golden roses she nurtures along the sea's edge, she bears new petals every day, her brightest colors peeking out after her worst days, her roots thriving even in ever-shifting soil.

The slippery feeling under her skin fades with time, but it will never fully be gone, and she would miss it just the same. For all its torture, for all the pinching and plucking and panicking, she would not be a warrior without its constant presence.

She will always be a warrior.

Though her lover stays by the sea, the warrior rose often returns south, to the scrublands where she was born.

The village has flourished, the hazel grove burgeoning ever-outward and the tulsi berries fattening more with each passing equinox. The bearsbane bushes will begin to flower soon, the villagers think, though they never have before. They sing songs in anticipation of such a marvel.

Though it still bears scars to remind the once-gods of divinity's shortcomings, and though one of its corners is still cast in horn-crowned shadow, the village's strength is in its people.

They are a strong, good people, and their festivities are unmatched.

The warrior rose does not mind so much that her past feats go unnoticed still. She's glad, now, that her title of Bearslayer was only ever used in friendliness. These people never intended for her to feel other, but they knew she wouldn't be dissuaded from the purpose she sought. She would have been one of them, if only she had allowed herself to be.

She partakes in their springtide celebrations, and at times she wishes she could have had this life—spinning children to dizziness, drinking herself silly, worrying for nothing but the eye of a potential husband. It would have been a simple life.

But simple is not what she was meant for.

At the heart of her visits to the scrublands, the warrior rose bares her skin to the healer's paints. They tease each other as her face is coated in greens and golds, and whisper softly of sadnesses shared as her arms are daubed in blue and silver. They never discussed the years spent apart, when each believed the other to be too far hurt for words, but they never needed to. Theirs was a special bond forged by brightness.

At moonswake, the warrior rose settles in a pile of furs with a bowl warming her palms. She's grown away from reliance on the tea's calming effects, but still enjoys the company of the boy with the horns.

She comes to realize that he's never been wild, not in the sense of a feral beast. He was wild in the sense that he always found his own way, such as life was intended. He learned from nature; he respected and nurtured it. When he saw pain, he soothed it. When he saw joy, he kindled it.

He would've been a good god, it was true. But she was glad he was this instead—she was glad he was her soothing thing.

So too does the warrior rose venture for a time to the mountain where the bees buzz their worries away, where a she-boar hunts mushrooms and a quiet man sends cartfuls of undrunk spirits to the lands below.

She helps him sow seeds in the neglected cliffside garden: fourteen rose bushes, hopeful gravemarkers that will flourish under the care of the staid, subdued once-god. He begins to sing again, his words a gentle magic. He no longer wishes for wings.

When she returns to the sea, the warrior rose stands before the ocean.

She sees its strength and its majesty, those things people always spoke of, but more closely she sees its openness; its vast, endless vulnerability. She sees the churning waves reaching for the sky, fighting to stay afloat, desperate for air. She sees the water crawling up the shore, urged forward by fear and shame, seeking escape from the overwhelming weight of its being.

She knows it could have chosen emptiness. She knows that would have been easier.

But emptiness would lend to nonexistence—the ocean couldn't be empty, or it wouldn't be an ocean.

Just as she knows love endures, she knows life is worth feeling.

Life is not nothing.

ACKNOWLEDGMENTS

I have endless depths of gratitude when it comes to *The Bear & the Rose*, and words can hardly convey the truth of how thankful I am for all the support I've received in crafting this tale.

Strange as it may seem, I first must express thanks for TB&TR itself as well as—in a strongly related way—my anxiety. I lost my sense of self in 2021, and this story and my mental health journey in no uncertain terms saved me. I learned so much about myself and my outlook on the world in penning this book, and I'm stronger and less ashamed for it. I am not weak by having debilitating anxiety, but rather strong because of it. I'm a godsdamned *warrior*, and I am meant to grow.

Infinite thanks to my family: your understanding and patience during this most difficult phase of my life is invaluable, and I am boundlessly grateful for it every day. Thank you for meeting my bouts of tears with only kindness, rather than questions or judgment. Thank you for responding to my last-minute messages of *I'm sorry, I just can't today* with only comfort, rather than anger or frustration. Thank you for never expecting words or explanations of my absence. Thank you for loving me all the same.

To my parents, especially: thank you for giving me everything.

I also owe much thanks to all my Bookstagram friends, to the indie authors forging the way, and to every writer who has borne their soul on paper. You are all *infinitely* inspiring, and without your bravery I may never have dusted off my old "plot bunnies" document and found the motivation to write again.

I don't believe in the star-system of rating books—no matter the quality of the words you put forth, they are priceless and important, and quantitative judgment means *nothing* in the scope of your talent. So keep writing. We're making a difference, I promise.

My next thanks comes with a surge of nostalgia as I recall all the teachers—starting with you, Mama, my first and greatest teacher—who kindled the flames of my creativity and taught me the way of storytelling. Mrs. Mathis, Professor Olson, Professor Veselis, Dr. Sabino, and especially Dr. Janet Lowery: no number of years will take away the deep amount of respect I hold for you all. I am proud to have learned from—and been critiqued and praised by—the best.

Thank you to my alpha readers, the first to give Rhoswen and me a chance. It was the most nerve-wracking moment sending my book baby off to be read by real, actual people, and I so appreciate the gentleness with which you all treated TB&TR.

Thank you, Brittany, for your wisdom, guidance, and calming nature. I am the hottest of all messes, and you have been a dream editor and a balm for my nervous baby author jitters. I am so delighted to call you a dear friend and to have had you on this journey with me.

Thank you, Mia, for your generous help with my pronunciation guide!

Thank you to all the artists who have brought my characters to life over the past year—Will Hatch, A.E. Jürgens, and Kim Carlika. I am amazed every day at the breadth of your talent as I look upon your renditions of Rhoswen and Dìomath. They could not be more perfect.

A HUGE thank-you to Nox Benedicta for my cover art. It is and will forever be beyond my wildest dreams, and your excitement, professionalism, and patience along the way made the experience truly and indescribably fulfilling. I sent you a novel of jumbled notes and you effortlessly swept them up and created a masterpiece worthy of the highest award.

Thank you, Andrew, for being my person. Thank you for helping me through my moments of panic, and for waking up in the wee hours of the morning when I couldn't breathe. Thank you for understanding my silences, and for urging me to prioritize myself. Thank you for never asking what my book is about because you knew it would make me feel awkward. Thank you for always making the coffee. Thank you for being my soothing thing.

And to Boosha: thank you for inspiring my interest in Celtic mythology, and for having been Septimus and Daaoud's first, biggest, and questionably only fan. Dragons will always remind me of you.

CPSIA information can be obtained
at www.ICGtesting.com
Printed in the USA
BVHW040202100523
663912BV00016B/95/J

9 781088 079980